PICKLED Petunia

DAHLIA DONOVAN

TANGLED TREE PUBLISHING

PICKLED PETUNIA

DAHLIA DONOVAN

TANGLED TREE PUBLISHING

For information, contact the publisher, Tangled Tree Publishing.

WWW.TANGLEDTREEPUBLISHING.COM

EDITING: Hot Tree Editing

COVER DESIGNER: BookSmith Design

E-book ISBN: 978-1-922359-96-4

PAPERBACK ISBN: 978-1-922359-97-1

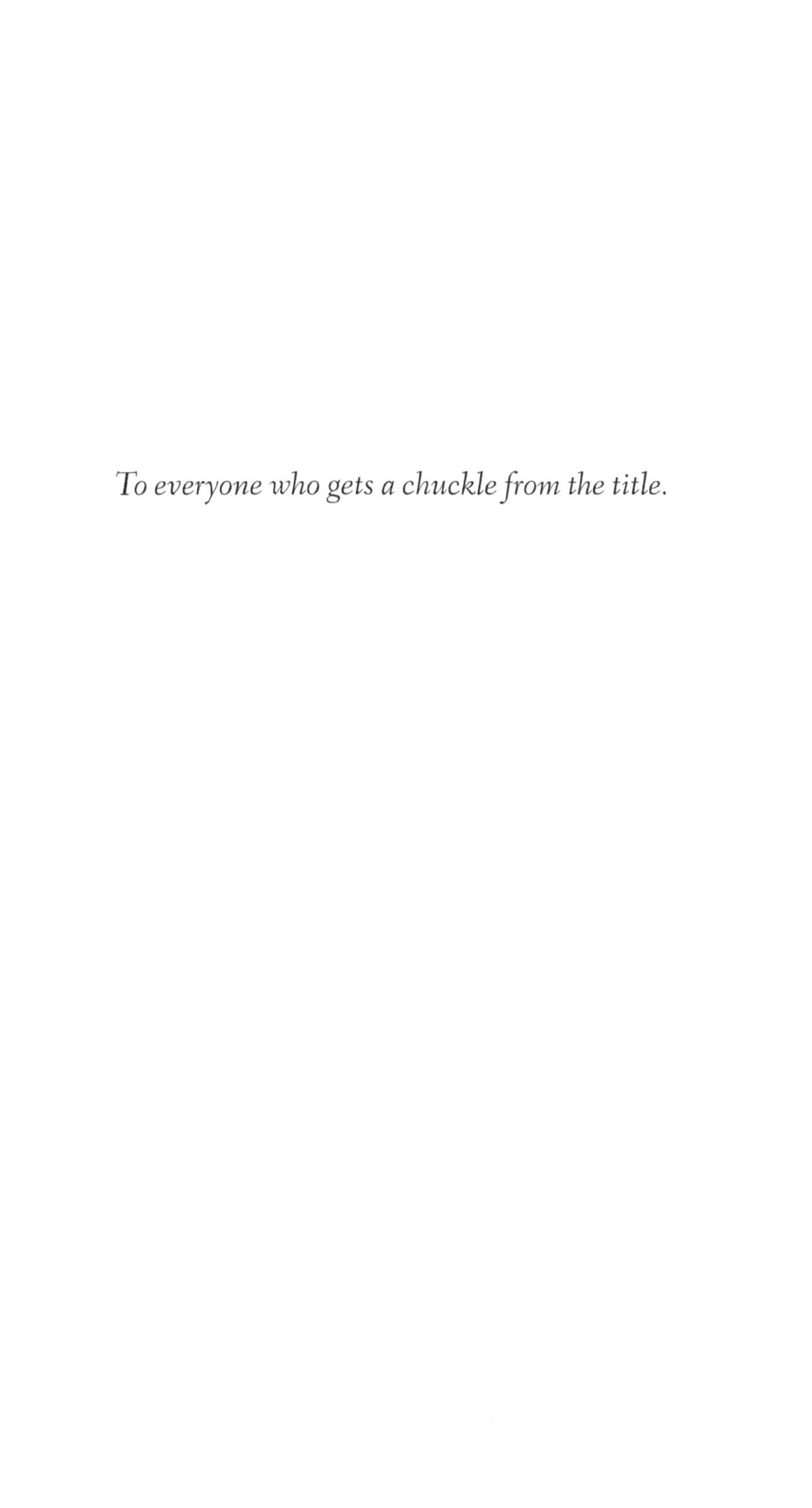

To everyone who gets a chuckle from the title.

CHAPTER ONE

A Pineapple, a cat, and a ruined brolly trudge into a cottage on a dreary October morning.

Motts loved autumn in Cornwall. Then again, she adored every season in her perfect little corner of the world. Polperro had become home.

Village life suited Pineapple Meg Mottley. She'd turned the small two-storey cottage, inherited from her auntie Daisy, into a cosy, warm space. Being up on a hill overlooking the village on one side and the sea on the other managed to offer a sense of privacy yet one of belonging as well.

Autumn in Cornwall involved many days of fighting with an umbrella. She'd attempted to go for a walk in the garden with Cactus, her tortoiseshell

Sphynx cat. He hadn't appreciated the sudden onslaught of wind and rain either.

Now she had a wet cat, a ruined umbrella, and a puddle of water leading through the living room.

Okay.

Fire. Must have warmth. And a towel. Cactus hissed his unhappiness from his favourite chair. He rolled around on the cushion, attempting to dry off his velvety soft fuzz.

It was only the two of them at home now. Moss, her twenty-year-old turtle, had been under the weather for weeks. Motts worried it missed its old stomping grounds in London.

After chatting with her vet and her parents, Motts had allowed them to take Moss home to London with them. She hoped it had the added benefit of helping her mum adjust to her lone daughter having flown the nest at the ripe old age of thirty-nine. One could always hope.

She missed Moss.

She didn't miss her mum's well-meaning yet suffocating attempts to care for her adult daughter.

It had started when she was a child. Motts had struggled at times, growing up, particularly in social situations. After the murder of her only school friend, Jenny, her mum had become unbearably overprotective. It hadn't changed throughout the years.

While her late autistic diagnosis had provided so many answers for Motts, her mum had taken it as evidence her daughter should stay home. The move to Cornwall hadn't done wonders for their relationship. Her dad told her not to worry.

He never worried.

Motts had inherited her father's brown hair, pale skin, and bluish-grey eyes. She'd also gotten his pragmatic streak and his distaste for confrontation. Her stubbornness, however, came straight from her mum.

Nine months of living on her own had improved her confidence and gone brilliantly—aside from two dead bodies and the criminal investigations that had followed. The last case had come to a dramatic conclusion at the end of summer; all had been quiet since then. Motts hoped the calm continued.

"Fire. I have made *fire*." Motts stood up and dusted off her knees. She adored having a hearth in the living room. It did wonders for the downstairs of the cottage. "Okay. Time for some hot chocolate. Want a snack, love?"

Meow.

Cactus immediately got comfortable on the cushion by the fireplace. It sat midway between the couch and the kitchen, offering him a view of Motts wherever she went. He was a delightfully spoiled cat.

"Settled in for the morning, are we?" Motts reached down to gently scratch his ears. "Do you want to wear your sweater?"

She eyed the knitted item draped across the arm of the sofa. *Teo.* Detective Inspector Herceg had officially moved away. Motts missed him as well.

The stern yet kind Teo had left several knitted sweaters for Cactus when he'd last visited. She thought the move had been harder for him than for her. Yet another sign, to her mind, their casual dating hadn't been destined for more.

Cat cardigan cuddles Cactus comfortably.

Motts was about to give herself ten points for a brilliant alliteration when the doorbell rang repeatedly. "Have I jinxed myself? Who's climbing up the hill on a dreary day like this?"

Grabbing her phone, Motts checked the app allowing her to spy through the doorbell. She thought the sodden young woman standing in the rain was familiar. *Where've I seen you?*

Halfway to the door, the answer struck Motts. *The Chinese-Cornish Business Association.* A group run by her auntie and uncle, Lily and Tom Chen-

Mottley. Her uncle Tomato had met Lily many years ago in Singapore during a university exchange program; the couple ran a Looe brewery with their son, River.

If Motts remembered correctly, the young woman at the door worked at another brewery in the area. They'd met once. Motts struggled with faces, though, particularly anyone outside of her close family and friends.

The doorbell rang again, several times.

"I should probably rescue her from the deluge." Motts went to answer the door. She didn't know what to say. "Hello."

That was normal, right?

"Can you find my mum?" her visitor blurted. "Please?"

That was definitely not normal.

Motts blinked a few times, trying to process the question shouted at her. "Pardon?"

"I should've called, shouldn't I?" She shoved damp hair out of her face. "Mikey said you're autistic and might appreciate a warning. I've just.... I'm desperate to find Mum. No one believes she's gone missing."

"I'm not the police." Motts flinched when a crack of thunder crashed overhead. "Okay. Come inside.

Everything makes more sense with a mug of tea. Mind the cat, he adopts strangers. Let me find you a towel."

"Cat?"

Motts waved her inside and pointed to the curious cat who'd come to investigate. "Cactus. Not prickly, mostly fuzzy. The kitchen's down there. I'll be a moment."

Why would Mikey give her my name?

Mikey O'Connell had been the grandson of a woman found floating in the sea in June. Motts had discovered his brother and mum were behind the horrific murder. They'd stayed in touch after the investigation.

Grabbing a towel from the upstairs bathroom, Motts returned to the kitchen. She put the kettle on, grabbed two mismatched mugs, and dropped two slices of bread in the toaster. Everything would hopefully make more sense after breakfast.

"Here." Motts offered the towel to her.

"Your auntie and my mum are great friends. I'm Paisley. Petunia Lee's my mum." She sat in the chair near the fire to dry off. Her whole body seemed to be shaking. "She works at one of the breweries near Looe. Her boyfriend said she left him a note saying she went on holiday."

"But?" Motts opted for one of the non-caffeinated teas her friend Vina had brought over for her. A lovely blackcurrant-flavoured one that reminded her strongly of Ribena. "Could she be on holiday?"

"Mum's not one to travel. I can't remember the last time she took a trip anywhere." Paisley began to towel dry her hair. She gratefully accepted the second one Motts handed to her. "She wouldn't go without telling me."

"Have you tried calling her? What about the police?" Motts wasn't sure how she could help. "I'm not a detective. I make origami bouquets and quilling art for a living. Don't think I'm the best first choice."

"The police said she's an adult. She can do what she wants." Paisley huffed in irritation. She wrapped the second towel around herself. "Mikey said you're great at solving mysteries."

Mikey's a liar.

And never invited to the cottage ever again.

"I'm mediocre at best. I can barely keep myself alive. I'm brilliant at origami." Motts carried the mugs over to the table. She went back to finish fixing up her breakfast of lemon curd on toast. Paisley sniffled into the towel. *I'm going to have to wash those. Empathy, Motts. She's obviously terri-*

fied for her mum. Don't do it. Don't. "How can I help?"

And there goes the peace and calm in the Mottley cottage.

Paisley wilted in front of her and gripped the mug tightly. "Thank you. Thank you. Thank you so much."

"You might want to wait until you see whether I accomplish anything at all." Motts nibbled on the edge of her toast. "Do you have the note she left?"

Paisley shook her head, causing the towel to loosen from around her head. "Could you come to the brewery? Her boyfriend—and mine, as well—works there."

"Tomorrow." Motts instantly regretted agreeing. She definitely wanted a day to process and prepare. Things already felt out of control. "I can ride over in the morning."

Mornings were good. Fewer people. Daylight. It would be safer. *What am I doing? Haven't I learnt anything over the past nine months?*

"I knew Mikey wouldn't steer me wrong." Paisley unwound the towels and draped them over the back of the chair. "I'll go home and change. Here's my number. Call me."

"I don't call. I text," Motts insisted. She did

wonder why Paisley hadn't spoken with her cousin River if Auntie Lily and Petunia Lee were such great friends.

The conversation ended awkwardly and quickly, with Paisley making her way out of the cottage. Motts shut the door, locked it, and rested her forehead against the wood. She could already hear the comments Teo would make about inserting herself into a potential investigation.

Except he's gone up north to be a proper detective inspector. What's the worst that can happen? Maybe River will go with me in the morning.

CHAPTER TWO

"Heard you had a visitor."

Motts considered closing the door on Vina before deciding it would be pointless. "Did you?"

Pravina Griffin, one of a trio of Motts's best friends and her ex-girlfriend, swanned into the cottage with her twin brother Nish and his boyfriend, River, trailing behind like wayward puppies. "We brought lamb biryani and curry pasties. Amma made your favourite rice for her favourite child."

Curry pasties were one of the specialities at Griffin Brews, the local Polperro bakery and coffee shop run by the twins and their parents, Cadan and Leena. The Cornish-Indian couple blended their cultures into the best fusion pastries in all Cornwall. Motts wasn't even close to exaggerating.

"Don't be daft." Motts shook her head at Vina's dramatics. "Why do I agree to host these get-togethers?"

"Because you like the comfort of your cottage." Nish lifted his arms and waited for Motts to decide if she wanted a hug. She did. "Plus, you enjoy being able to chuck us out if Vina gets on your nerves."

"Hello, young Pineapple." River mimicked his dad's voice perfectly. "Mum made a batch of shepherd's pie baos for us."

Once a week, the four friends got together at the cottage to watch YouTube videos. Recently, Vina's new girlfriend, Taara Khatri, had joined them when she wasn't travelling for her family's import/export business. Motts thought she made an excellent addition to their group.

If nothing else, Taara had an amazing calming effect on Vina. Motts was thrilled her best friend/ex-girlfriend had found love. Now, if she'd stop trying to find it for Motts, everything would be perfect.

While River got to work setting up the playlist, Vina followed Motts into the kitchen with the tray of food. Cactus immediately raced up to her. Vina lifted him up to lavish attention on the purring feline.

"Heard from Teo recently?" Vina leant against the counter. "Is Detective Inspector Tall, Dark, and Brooding coming for a visit from Yorkshire?"

"Vina."

"Mottsy," Vina cajoled. "Nothing from him at all?"

"We email. It's quite friendly." Motts believed the door had closed on any chance of a romantic relationship with Teo. "We're moving on. Both of us."

"Excellent."

Motts was immediately suspicious of the sudden change. She pulled the plates down from the cupboard and set them on the counter. "No."

"I haven't said anything." Vina proclaimed her innocence, setting Cactus on the floor and coming over to grab the plates. "I've met—"

"No," Motts repeated firmly. "You're not setting me up on a date."

"I'm hurt at your lack of faith and trust in me." Vina ignored the snorts from Motts, Nish, and River. "You'd like Beck. They're lovely."

"Beck?"

"Have you seen the Ferris Wheel? The new gastropub. It moved into where the used bookshop used to be." River poked his nose into the conversation. "They're the chef and owner."

"Ferris?" Motts had seen the new restaurant. "Any relation to Doc and Elys?"

Carridoc and Elys Ferris ran the Polperro post office. They were a lovely older couple who'd helped Motts after a road accident. She tried to stop by to see them once a week.

"Their grandchild." Nish eased the lid off the container with the pasties. "Beckett Ferris. They moved from Paris after working in some fancy restaurant."

"And they had their heart broken in France," Vina added.

"Is there anything local gossip can't discover?" Motts was always amazed by the power of the village grapevine.

"No one knows why Paisley Lee drove from Looe to visit you while looking like a drenched seagull." River spoke around the bao in his mouth. "So? What did she want? Mum didn't even know, and she's best friends with Auntie Petunia."

And so commences the semi-annual meeting of the worst amateur detectives in Cornwall.

They'll vote us most likely to get ourselves killed before the year is over.

Curling up on the sofa with a plate of food, Motts filled her friends in on what little she'd gotten from Paisley. There hadn't been a tonne of details. They didn't even know if Petunia Lee had gone missing.

"I'm going to ask Mum. She's been friends with Petunia for ages. Think they even went to the same school in Singapore." River dug into his pocket for his phone. "We'll have everything but her birth certificate by the time Mum's finished."

Auntie Lily prided herself on being thorough. Motts wouldn't be surprised if she did find them a copy of her birth certificate. The whole Looe community would be on the lookout for Petunia, which might help find her.

If she was missing.

They didn't get around to watching the videos they had lined up for the evening. Instead, they formulated a plan for the following day. River had agreed to go with her to visit the brewery; he'd pick her up to save a potentially rainy journey for her.

Motts had three modes of transportation. Her 3-Speed Pure City Crosby Classic bicycle, a seafoam green Vespa scooter, and walking. It usually got her where she wanted to go, but rainy days weren't as fun for her.

"Listen." Vina remained by the door after Nish and River had already headed to the car. "About Beckett Ferris."

Motts rubbed her cheek against Cactus's head. "Will you stop trying to set me up on dates?"

"Nope." Vina dropped a kiss on Motts's forehead and then one on Cactus. "Pop by in the morning for coffee and a croissant."

"Vina."

"What?" She grinned innocently. "Seven's the perfect time. You'll be able to relax and have breakfast before River pops by to pick you up."

With a belaboured sigh, Motts waved goodbye to her friends. She retreated into the cottage with Cactus. When Vina had an idea, she tended to want to see it through.

She'll get bored eventually and move on to something else.

Or I can bribe Leena to rein her daughter in a little.

"Bath time?" Motts laughed when Cactus immediately leapt out of her arms. "I won't throw you in the water. I promise. Poor little warrior."

Sinking into the hot water twenty minutes later, Motts tried to organise her thoughts. *Am I ready for another mystery?* The last two had almost gotten her killed.

"We'll work harder this time to avoid close encounters of the cliff kind." Motts eyed Cactus purring by the door. "And yes, I'll make sure the alarm is set and the doors are locked."

And I won't mention this to Teo in our next email. He might warn whoever the new detective inspector in Plymouth might be.

Ten minutes into her bath, Motts shot up out of the tub. She'd overheated. It was always so difficult to get the temperature right.

She tended to go from fine to heatstroke in mere seconds.

Meow.

"Yes, Cactus. I'm done drowning myself." Motts stretched out on her stomach on the cold tile floor, breathing slowly. "Just give me a second."

One of these days, I'll learn not to slowly boil myself in the bath.

Probably not.

Taking her bathrobe off the hook by the door, Motts wrapped herself up in it. She padded through the cottage into her bedroom. Cactus followed, making himself comfortable on her pillow.

Motts sank into the armchair by the bed. "What am I going to do?"

Cactus, as always, didn't offer any words of wisdom.

"Maybe we'll find Petunia sunning herself on a beach somewhere." Motts didn't believe that would be the case. "I've a terrible feeling something dreadful has happened to her."

Or, maybe, stumbling across two dead bodies this year has jaded me a little.

CHAPTER THREE

"You're having a panic attack. I'll sit here, nattering on to myself. You keep counting your breaths." The stranger sat on the kerb beside Motts, leaving some space between them. "Just keep going. In and out."

This is so embarrassing.

The morning had started well. Early, but fine. Motts had ridden her bicycle down to Griffin Brews, leaving it locked up behind the café. Vina had obviously had far too much espresso; she immediately peppered her with questions about a potential date with Beck.

Caught up in preparing herself for a day with River and Paisley, Motts had reeled from the onslaught of questions. She'd spiralled quickly into an anxiety attack. It had culminated in her rushing from the café, trying to remember how to breathe.

Breathe in, one-two-three-four, out, one-two-three-four. In, one-two-three-four, out, one-two-three-four.

I'm safe. I'm fine. I'm exhausted.

It took what seemed like ages for her breathing to return to normal. Motts was exhausted and embarrassed. She wanted to just run home and hide from the world for a few days.

She glanced over at the stranger, a person who appeared about her age with short, thick black hair and brown eyes. They wore tight black jeans, black boots, and a hoodie. "Hello."

"Morning." They held out a paper sack toward Motts. "Fizzy cola bottle? Picked some up at the sweet shop. I'm Beck, by the way."

Motts grabbed a handful, popping one in her mouth. "Pineapple Mottley. Almost everyone calls me Motts."

"My grandparents told me about you. Beckett Ferris. Or just Beck, as I mentioned." They tossed a sweet into their mouth. "My roommate, when I lived in Paris, used to have panic attacks at least once a week."

"Sounds exhausting." Motts ate another one of the sweets.

"Listen. I'm aware Pravina wanted to introduce us. Granny and Granddad mentioned you as well." Beck dragged fingers through their short, slicked-back hair. "The joys of village living. Suppose I'll get used to it. No one in Paris was ever bothered to introduce themselves, let alone someone else."

Motts covered her face with her hands and groaned in added embarrassment. "Not sure sitting on a dirty kerb while I panic was how they hoped we'd meet."

How on earth am I going to deal with Paisley and hunting around for clues about where her mum went?

"Want to talk?"

"We are talking." Motts peeked between her fingers to find Beck grinning. "Right? Not imagining this."

"Literal thinker, eh?"

"Autistic." Motts shrugged. "Literal thinking comes with the territory."

"Sweet."

Motts didn't think she'd ever received that response from someone. "Okay."

"Well, I'm Beck. I don't enjoy long walks on the beach. Sand sticks to everything. Cooking is my life." They smiled at Motts again. "I'm also a shit baker."

"Motts. Love the ocean. Not fussed about sand.

Brilliant at origami. Shit at many other things." Motts found herself calming down around the mild energy surrounding Beck. "Proud human of Cactus the cat who rules the universe."

"I have to go cook things, since the restaurant won't run itself. You've got papers to fold. Come by the Ferris Wheel sometime, yeah? I'll cook up something special for you." Beck winked at her, then got to their feet. They dropped the sack of candy in Motts's lap. "Here. Enjoy the rest on me."

Motts sat in silence for a few minutes, eating her way through far too many sweets. She heard a familiar musical laugh behind her.

"Morning. Straying away from your baking?"

"My Vina's most apologetic." Leena joined Motts on the kerb. She patted Motts gently on the knee. "She was overexcited and will find you later. My Nish will bring you one of our new tea blends. Calming, sweetly spiced. We've also made a batch of curried English breakfast pasties. You'll want at least two, since your cousin is likely to steal one from you."

Before Motts could respond, Leena had returned to the café. She swanned off with the air of the Bollywood princess she'd been. It was always so easy to see how Caden had fallen in love with her.

Getting to her feet, Motts brushed off her jeans.

Vina probably did feel awful. It was hard to resist the urge to rush into the café to reassure her.

I didn't do anything wrong. I'm allowed to be overwhelmed by a barrage of high energy and questions. Vina (and our friendship) will survive a small dose of guilt and self-reflection.

Guilty grimacing guides... I've run out of g's.

"Hello, Nish." Motts nodded awkwardly when he stepped out of the café.

"Hello, fruity one. Our best brew. Three pasties plus a selection of our new autumn-themed macarons. You'll enjoy the sweet curry pumpkin one, in particular, I think. Plus, there's a salted caramel cashew one as well." Nish offered her a reusable travel mug and the box of treats. "River's parked down the street having a chat with Hughie about the new detective inspector coming to replace Teo."

Constable Hughie Stone was a local lad. He'd been born and raised in Cornwall by his grandparents, who'd immigrated from Jamaica. He'd helped Motts in her garden this past spring.

Motts wandered down the pavement towards her cousin, sipping the warm tea and almost immediately feeling a little better. "Is it a placebo if it works because I believe it will?"

"Mottsy." River greeted her with a smile. He

nodded toward the constable. "Hughie's got a crush on the new detective inspector who's moving to Plymouth."

Hughie sent a withering glare to River before offering a more friendly glance to Motts. "Detective Inspector Yuen went to school with me. She's a brilliant officer and chuffed to be returning home to Cornwall."

"And he's got a crush," River teased.

"If you're quite finished, what are you two up to this morning?" Hughie accepted one of the macarons when Motts held the box out to him. "See you've already popped into the café."

What are we doing? We can't tell him the truth. Oh no.

"We're going on a tour of breweries in the area. A little research." River smoothly filled the silence while Motts flailed for something to say. "My mum asked me to go."

"And Motts?" Hughie turned to her. "Expanding your Hollyhock Blooms business to include hops?"

"I'm moral support." Motts climbed into the passenger side of her cousin's car. "Lovely to see you, Constable. We don't want to be late for our first appointment. Bye."

River started the car and pulled away from the

kerb. He waited until they'd driven out of Polperro to interrupt her quiet breakfast. "He's probably even more curious now than he was before."

"As long as he stays curious in Polperro, we'll be fine." Motts finished up the breakfast pasty and offered the second one to River when he held his hand out. "Did Auntie Lily manage to discover anything?"

"Other than a hole in Dad's sock?"

"What?" Motts stared at him.

"Joke."

"How is a hole in a sock a joke? There's no punchline." Motts was even more confused.

"As in, I was joking. Never mind. It's not important." River brushed pastry flakes off his shirt.

"But how is it funny?"

River cleared his throat a few times before grabbing for his own travel mug and taking a long sip. "I was being silly. Mum hasn't heard anything from Mrs Lee. She said they usually chat fairly frequently."

Motts decided to leave the bizarre not-joke alone and focus on the more pressing mystery. "No response from Petunia Lee at all?"

"None. Mum said she always answers her phone." River reached over to grab one of the macarons. "She's worried. Thinks Paisley should ring the police again."

"Paisley perfectly punts priorities."

"Not your best alliteration work." River frowned when she closed the lid on the treats. "Rude."

"You don't get to insult my alliteration and steal my breakfast." Motts clutched the box to her chest. "Will your mum call the police?"

"I imagine she'll hound them until they at least do a welfare check on her." River paused to rudely insult the lorry who cut him off. "She's going to wait until we've done our investigation this morning."

"Think we'll really find something?" Motts didn't have a lot of faith in their abilities. Her previous two investigations had been solved more accidentally than on purpose. "And what do you know about Paisley?"

"We might find something. Who knows?" He shrugged. "She's petite. A lot like my mum, except she's not quite so intense. We're not friends, not really. She's a few years younger than me. She wanted out of Cornwall. I was surprised she moved back. She had a falling out with her mum."

"Did she?" Motts glanced over at him in surprise. "Not the impression I got."

From their brief conversation, Motts had thought

Paisley and her mum got along well. Hadn't Teo mentioned killers sometimes report crimes to appear innocent? Was trying to find Petunia a cover for hiding a murder?

Motts decided to wait until they'd snooped around to come to any conclusions. "Do you know Detective Inspector Yuen?"

"Not well. Rebecca Yuen. She, like Paisley, tried to escape our small village life. The Chinese community here is really close. All our mums know each other." River had never been overly bothered by his tight relationship with his family. He was too laid-back to be. "I'm honestly surprised she's returning. Maybe her crush on Hughie brought her home."

"River."

"What?"

"We're not matchmaking the local constable and the returning detective inspector." Motts didn't think Hughie's generally jovial nature would stretch to ignoring their interfering in his romantic life. "Let him manage on his own."

"He's not managing. When did he last go on a date?"

"This is a bizarre conversation, and I am no longer taking part in it." Motts turned her head to stare at the car in front of them. They should've timed their trip better to avoid morning traffic. "Did Paisley ask you about me?"

"No. You're not really thinking she did her mum in." River honked his horn when a vehicle swerved towards them. He paused to throw a few choice words at the driver. "Mottsy?"

"Stranger things have happened." Motts couldn't help thinking of poor Mikey's grandmother and the murderous family history that led to his mum and grandmother being murdered. Jasper, his brother, wasn't likely to be released from prison anytime soon. "We should keep our minds open to all possibilities."

"Murder's making you paranoid."

"Can you blame me?" Motts offered him one of the last macarons. "Murder makes Motts moderately…."

"You ran out of m-words."

"Just drive." She rolled her eyes at his ridiculousness.

"Yes, mistress. Anything you say, mistress."

"There's an m-word." Motts shifted in the seat, jumping slightly when her phone buzzed in her pocket. She often considered throwing the thing into the sea for all the stress it brought. "Why's Dempsey texting me?"

"Ooh, the fancy London detective inspector sending love notes." River, on occasion, did an excellent impression of a twelve-year-old. "Well? What's it say?"

"It says my cousin is a childish prat who didn't deserve the last macaron." Motts stuck her tongue out at him. "He can't know what we're doing, can he?"

"Not unless he's psychic."

Dempsey Byrne was a cold case detective with the Metropolitan Police in London. A few months ago, he'd come to Polperro to speak with her. Jenny's unsolved murder had been reopened.

He was impossibly tall, like Teo. Then again, anyone over six feet felt like a giant to Motts. He'd had more of a twinkle in his eye than the more stoically serious Teo.

The case had never been solved. Motts still remembered the day she stumbled across the body of her friend in a park. It was etched in her mind.

Jenny's body had been shoved under a bush. Motts had recognised her coat. She'd never forgotten the loss.

"What's he say?"

"They've discovered more girls from my class are missing or were found dead in mysterious circumstances." Motts's fingers trembled around her phone. "He's on his way from London."

River reached out to grip her hand gently. "You'll be fine."

"I'm not so sure." Motts couldn't get her fingers to work to send a response to Dempsey. She pocketed her phone, deciding to reply later. "Are we there yet?"

"Not quite."

CHAPTER FOUR

Coastal Port Brewery was surprisingly not near the Looe port. It sat outside of the village. The property had once been a large farm; the buildings had been converted to suit the business of making beer.

"Why call it Coastal Port Brewery?" Motts sat up straighter, noticing the large sign at the start of the narrow lane leading to the parking area.

"The original building by the coast burnt down in 1912 or something. I don't remember. They moved it further out of the village. The Port family sold the business about twenty years ago." River shrugged. He eased the car into the employee parking next to Paisley, who stood next to a sporty little Porsche. "Fancy."

"I'm so glad you made it." Paisley stammered to a halt when she spotted Motts's cousin getting out of the driver seat. "River?" She shook herself, then refocused on Motts. "The brewery doesn't open to the public for a few hours, so our timing is perfect. Louis said to check out Mum's office."

"Louis?" River asked.

"My boyfriend. His parents own the brewery." Paisley waited while they got themselves sorted. "It's been in their family for years now."

"Do you work at the brewery?" Motts followed Paisley up the stone path toward what had once been a large barn. "Was this all part of the farm?"

"The Ports converted the property to a distillery, keeping the façade of the farmhouse and barns. The renovations took forever." Paisley pulled a ring of keys out of her pocket. "Ready? I'll give you a little tour on the way up to her office."

Motts stared up at the multiple storey building. It looked like a stylised Victorian version of a barn at a commercial farm, based on the size. "Quite the warehouse."

"When Louis's parents took over twenty years ago, they expanded the distillery. Mum came on board to help. It was her idea to add a tasting area along with a gift shop. The tours helped keep the brewery afloat during tough times." Paisley motioned for them to follow her inside. "And yes, I help out part-time. I run the social media presence."

River glanced back at the Porsche and nudged Motts. He bent down to whisper, "Part-time with a car like hers?"

Motts shoved him away from her ear. She followed Paisley through a narrow hallway and up two flights of stairs. The offices ran along the outside of the building, offering views into the working distillery on the ground floor. "Do you enjoy being here with your mum and boyfriend? Must be challenging."

"It can be." Paisley flipped light switches as they went. She eventually led them to a closed door. "Mum's office. She's essentially in charge of running the brewery. Louis's still at university. He'll take over when he graduates."

Interesting.

So the boyfriend's in line to be in charge, but Petunia's doing a brilliant job?

The office was impressive. A wall of windows on one side offered a view across the ground floor below. Everything in the office was neatly organised, not a paper out of place.

Paisley immediately went over to the desk. She

shifted through the papers in the outbox, ruining the neat stack. "Nothing about her going out of town."

"Did she have a calendar?" Motts glanced around the room. "Smells like chocolate. Honey and chocolate."

"You're smelling the malt." River stopped inspecting a row of photos on the right wall. "Our brewery tends towards roasted malts with a hint of coffee flavour and a sweet caramel aroma. We play with spices more than the Coastal Port brew does. Though, they also make absinthe where we stick to beer instead of dabbling into liquors."

"Absinthe was Louis's brainchild. He works with the brewmaster on it. Here." Paisley laid out the large planner, pushing the keyboard and mouse out of the way. She tapped her finger against three of the squares. "Meetings. She's missed two of them. Mum cared too much about the brewery to blow off a profitable business connection."

Flipping through the past few weeks in the daily planner, Motts arrived at two obvious conclusions. First, Petunia Lee organised her life down to the minute. Second, she would never have gone off without leaving behind some evidence.

A person like Petunia didn't wander off at the drop of a hat. She wasn't going to blow off a business appointment. Impulsive wouldn't have been in her vocabulary.

If I'm right, and she didn't go off on a spontaneous holiday, where is she?

"Is her office always so...." River didn't seem to know how to finish the sentence.

"Sterile?" Motts offered.

"Motts." River covered his face with his hand. "I was trying to think of a kinder word."

"Why?" Motts didn't see the point of dancing around the obvious. She could've run a white-gloved finger across every surface in the office without finding a single speck of dust. "Paisley knows her mum better than we do. Sterile is probably kinder than what she's thought about it."

"Motts," River groaned.

"Is this one of those weird neurotypical things where we're supposed to pretend the obvious isn't obvious?" Motts tugged at the collar of her cardigan. It felt tight around her neck. "There's no dust anywhere."

"Mikey mentioned you weren't always socially adept." Paisley interrupted her muttered argument with River.

"Yes." Motts peered around the room one more

time. She used her phone to take a video of it along with the calendar. "I'm going outside."

Moving quickly down through the eerily quiet warehouse, Motts made her way out to the employee parking. Even in the crisp, damp air, she struggled with a tightening in her chest. She wrapped her arms around herself and began walking down the gravel lane leading out of the brewery.

It took a while to make it to Station Road. She continued down into Looe. River caught up to her when she'd almost reached the stile at the start of the Looe to Polperro walking path.

"Motts."

"Don't want to talk." She didn't glance at him.

"We don't have to say a word. Just let me give you a lift." River drove beside her at a crawl. "Come on."

"I want quiet," Motts insisted stubbornly.

"Dad's going to kill me." River had to stop at the end of the road. "Please?"

"Go home." Motts manoeuvred around the stile onto the path.

Leaving her cousin behind, Motts trudged along a narrow path beyond the stile. She breathed in deeply, the salty sea air boosting her spirits a little.

Well, what a horrid start to the day; it can only go up from here. I hope.

While a two-hour hike hadn't been part of her plan for the day, Motts decided to make the most of it. She loved Cornwall in the autumn. With cooler weather and fewer tourists, all her favourite walking paths became far less crowded.

It also gave her time to think about the disastrous end to their first visit to the brewery. River sometimes didn't understand how her mind processed things. And to be fair to him, there were loads of times he confused her just as much.

An hour into her walk, Motts had thought of a thousand better ways to handle the conversation at the brewery. She also wished her cup wasn't still sitting in River's car. Life never seemed quite so complex with a tea.

When Motts reached one of the high points along the cliffs, she found a large rock off the dirt path and climbed up to rest. Grey clouds cast a shadowy glint across the rough seas. The churning waves matched her turbulent thoughts.

No point in berating myself or River.

Miscommunications were always going to happen.

Ten minutes from home, a slight mist off the sea

turned into a downpour. Motts arrived at the cottage soaked through. She came around the corner to find a familiar vehicle parked in the driveway.

"Gran. Granddad." Motts fumbled with her keys before getting the door open and waving her grandparents inside. "What brings you out on a rainy day?"

"Go change into something cosy, poppet." Her grandmother patted her damp cheeks gently. "I'll get the kettle going for you."

"We brought you half of your gran's famous cherry Bakewell loaf." Her granddad bent down to pick up Cactus, who'd immediately raced over to him. "Morning, young man. Are you treating my granddaughter well? Oh, and I've brought some seeds for your garden. We want to get ready for winter. Well? Go get changed. Don't keep my Martha waiting."

"Granddad."

"Don't worry, poppet. We're not camping out for the day." He ushered her toward the stairs leading up to her bedroom. "We've only come to get lunch for you and share our love with Cactus."

Not having words to respond, Motts nodded and attempted a grateful smile. She climbed the stairs to her bedroom. Her uncle Tom had probably called in her grandparents when River returned to the family brewery.

They tended to be the calmest members of the family. Her uncle and auntie were lovely but demonstrated love with a lot of hugging. Motts didn't want or need to be crowded after a morning like she'd had.

Stepping into her bedroom and closing the door, Motts stripped out of her wet clothes. She dug out her comfiest and warmest pyjamas. Changing into them, she also grabbed the warm hooded dressing gown that Vina had bought for her last Christmas.

She returned downstairs to find a fire already cheerily brightening her living room. Cactus was lounging on the sofa with her granddad. She could hear her grandmother humming away in the kitchen.

Motts fluffed her wet hair with her fingers and flopped into the armchair by the fire. "You're spoiling him."

"Me?" Her granddad didn't look up from where he was feeding a treat to a purring Cactus. "I found these in the kitty cupboard in your kitchen."

"Rude of you to point out my hypocrisy." Motts glanced up when her grandmother came into the living room with a tray. "Gran?"

"Here's a mug of tea, some cake, and a few slices of toast with your lemon curd." Her grandmother set the tray on the coffee table in front of her. She bent down to kiss Motts on the forehead. "You relax by the fire for a while, poppet. We're going for lunch at the café to catch up with Leena and Caden."

Motts tried not to tear up in front of her grandparent. "Thanks, Gran."

Some days, family and friends were the best part of having moved from London to Polperro.

CHAPTER FIVE

"WE NEED TO RESTART THE DAY." MOTTS PEERED out the living room window to see the rain had stopped and the sun was out. She picked Cactus up. "How about an adventure in the garden?"

Out in the garden where it's nice and safe. No one to bother me. And no apologies to be made or received. Meow.

"Yes, I agree. Being in the garden is one of the best ways to spend an afternoon." Motts decided to make space in her makeshift greenhouse for the seeds her granddad had brought. "Don't eat any leaves."

The rain had left the soil damp. Motts spent time with her dirt, getting the seeds settled into tiny pots in her greenhouse.

In September, her granddad and Hughie had come over to help her remove the shed. They built a more functional one that did double duty as a greenhouse and potting shed, while also having space for storage.

Motts wished she didn't have terrible allergies. She would've loved to include flowers amongst the vegetables, fruits, and herbs to brighten up her garden. Though, harvesting tomatoes and shallots at the beginning of autumn had been a wonderful supplement to her groceries.

"Right." Motts finished pottering around with the little seeds and set them along one of the shelves in the greenhouse. "I could do with some fish and chips."

Meow.

"Yes, you always fancy fish. Let's get you inside where it's warm and dry." Motts had spent longer than intended in the garden. She headed toward the cottage with Cactus following close behind. "You're overdue a nap."

Sometimes after a meltdown or shutdown, Motts would lose hours out of her day. It was already after six. She still felt utterly mentally drained.

Once inside, Cactus immediately leapt up onto his fluffy bed. Motts had placed it where Moss's terrarium used to sit by the window facing the garden. He rested his head against a turtle plushie; the toy had been a gift from her uncle Tom.

A joke, Motts thought, except Cactus loved it.

Changing out of her dirt-covered clothes, Motts decided to walk into the village instead of cycling. It was a lovely, crisp autumn afternoon. She grabbed one of her thicker cardigans on her way outside.

Motts paused after locking the door. She peered around, taking in the magnificent view of Polperro from above. The narrow streets, the stark white buildings clustered together, the harbour with loads of fishing boats moored in the mud, waiting for high tide the following morning. *This is home. It's not hard to see why Auntie Daisy lived here all of her life. It's a little piece of heaven.*

With one final look and a deep, calming breath, Motts carefully made her way down the narrow, steep stairs leading into the village. She waved to Doc and Elys, who were closing up the post office for the evening. They waited for her to cross the street and join them.

"Hello, ducky." Doc smiled over his shoulder, then went back to fussing with the lock. "Hope you've got a working brolly. We're in for rain again. I can feel it in my big toe."

"Really?" Motts asked, intrigued.

"Ignore him, love. He's an old grump who fancies his toe an accurate gauge of the weather." Elys enjoyed teasing her husband. She nudged him and took the keys out of his hand. "Picking up something for tea?"

"I promised Cactus fish and chips." Motts tried to ease out of the conversation. She never knew how to withdraw from discussions without feeling rude or awkward. "The Salty Seaman should still be open."

The Salty Seaman was a Polperro staple. It served the best fish and chips in the area. Motts had slowly been gaining the courage to go in on her own.

Her introduction to Innis and Rose, who ran the restaurant, hadn't been brilliant. She'd all but accused them of killing his sister, whose body had been found in Motts's garden. An easy mistake to make. They did seem to have finally forgiven her.

"You should visit our Beck's Ferris Wheel." Elys ignored her husband tugging on her coat. "They have wonderful fish and chips there."

"Ignore my old matchmaker. Go get your food." Doc winked at her.

Leaving the couple to bicker about their grandchild's dating life, Motts continued down the street. She didn't want gastropub fare. Fish and chips tasted different wrapped in paper and doused with salt, vinegar, and ketchup.

Motts stood across the street from the Salty Seaman, trying to talk herself into going inside. "You can do this. You're only going to get food. Then you can hibernate all evening with Cactus. Innis doesn't glare as much as he used to."

"They say talking to yourself is a sign of genius."

"Do they?" Motts glanced over her shoulder to find Detective Inspector Byrne stepping out of the restaurant behind her. "Hello. When did you arrive?"

"An hour ago. I took the scenic route." Dempsey stepped up beside her. "Hughie's kindly allowed me to crash in his spare room while I'm here. Lovely chap. Are you planning to storm the Bastille? Want reinforcements?"

"You're always here when I'm facing my fears." Motts remembered when he'd first shown up to talk about Jenny's case. He'd helped her find the courage to walk the coastal path after she'd almost gone off the cliff. "I suppose reinforcements can't hurt."

Dempsey held his arm up for her. "Ready?"

Motts glanced at his arm, then at his chin, because eye contact was too much at the moment. She ignored him and walked across the street. "I'm relatively certain Innis won't cause a scene. He grunted at me the other day. Almost friendly."

"We've got to raise your standards on customer service at restaurants."

"They're not throwing rocks through my windows. And they don't shout anymore." Motts considered it a massive improvement. "Are you going to tell me why you're here?"

"Tomorrow." Dempsey grabbed the door and held it open for her. "You seem at capacity today."

Once inside the Salty Seaman, Motts spotted Innis behind the counter. He grunted once and immediately began portioning out three fish and a handful of chips into a packet. Dempsey chuckled behind her.

"Come here often?"

Motts chose to ignore the glowering Innis and the bemused detective. Her mission was fish and chips. She gratefully accepted the packet held out across the counter. "Thank you."

Walking, not running, out of the chippy, Motts started toward home. Dempsey caught up with her. He walked on the street, given the narrow pavement.

"Why are you here?" Motts's curiosity and anxiety combined to potent effect. She couldn't imagine he'd shown up for a vacation. "Did you find the killer?"

"Motts." Dempsey caught her arm to stabilise her when she tripped over a crack in the pavement. "Easy there. It'll keep until morning."

Oh yes, plenty of time for me to drive myself up the wall imagining every possible scenario.

Scary scenarios steal safety.

Climbing the long, narrow steps up the hill, Motts tried to enjoy the late autumn evening. Dempsey followed her all the way to her cottage. He didn't come inside when she opened the door.

"Not staying?"

"I've promised Inspector Ash I'd swing around to chat with him about a case." Dempsey crouched down to pet a purring Cactus. "Love the cardigan."

"A gift from Teo." Motts shrugged.

"Ah yes, your detective inspector."

"Not mine. People aren't possessions." She shifted her fish and chips to her other hand. "And not here anymore."

"Interesting." Dempsey gave Cactus one last rub on the head. "Why don't I swing by tomorrow? I'll bring lunch. And try not to stress. There are a few questions I wanted to ask in person."

"Right." Motts watched him saunter off down the lane, whistling to himself.

Meow.

"Yes, yes. You've conquered another detective inspector. Stop gloating." Motts nudged the purring Cactus gently with her toe until he moved enough for her to close the door. She carried her dinner through to the kitchen. "Why don't I plate this up? We can watch Tingting and relax by the fire."

Flaky fish, salty chips, and relaxing ASMR.

Flaky fish for felines.

Motts set up one of Tingting's playlists and began picking through her dinner. She offered Cactus bites of the fish without batter, and the cat eventually curled up in her lap. "What do you think Dempsey wants?"

Cactus shuffled further into her lap.

"I agree. He's definitely found something." Motts tried to settle into a shampooing video. Her mind wouldn't stop considering the options.

Even her favourite ASMR YouTube channel couldn't fully relax Motts. She kept thinking about Jenny's death. Why else would Dempsey be in Cornwall again? What had he discovered?

Oh yes, I'm definitely going to relax with this hanging over my head.

CHAPTER SIX

THE SUN HADN'T RISEN WHEN MOTTS WOKE UP the following day. She turned off her alarm an hour before it was supposed to go off. Days were already starting to feel shorter.

"We're going to have a better day." Motts carefully placed Cactus onto a pillow while she made up the rest of the bed. She tugged gently on the soft quilt, a gift from her grandmother. "Ready, Cactus? How about an early breakfast?"

A contented meow was her only response. Motts wrapped her dressing gown around her and headed downstairs with Cactus following close behind. After getting his first meal of the day ready, she had a simple breakfast of tea and lemon curd on toast for herself.

Cactus had a high metabolism that required little snacks throughout the day.

He also required a lot of attention.

Turning on one of her favourite YouTube channels, Motts got a fire going, then started work. Her origami bouquet and quilling art business, Hollyhock Folded Blooms, had been doing reasonably well online. She'd also gotten loads of commissions from Marnie Ash, who ran the local bridal shop.

Her current project was one from Marnie. A collection of bouquets for a bridal party. She had a week to make seven of them. Setting all of her papers and equipment on the kitchen table, Motts got to folding.

After several hours, Motts had an army of deep purple, burgundy, merlot, and forest green flowers and leaves. She was more than ready for a hot chocolate break when someone knocked on the door. *I should get a Do Not Disturb sign and hang it outside on days when I can't be bothered by social interaction.*

Maybe Dempsey's here early to chat about Jenny's case.

Motts pulled up her doorbell app on her phone only to find Paisley once again outside her cottage. "Why is she here?"

Meow.

"No, I won't know unless I answer the door. Good point." Motts pocketed her phone and went to greet Paisley. She appeared far more demure with a small car and simple jeans and cardigan, far less flashy than the day before. "Hello."

"I brought scones and tea." Paisley held up a basket with the aforementioned scones and a resealable bag of some sort of dried blend. "Perhaps we could start over? I'm not sure where the conversation went wrong yesterday."

Neither am I.

I'm going to have to invite her inside.

I don't want to invite her inside.

"Why don't you come... inside?" Motts almost spit out the last word. Paisley was an unexpected visitor. She'd only practised conversations with Dempsey while in the shower. "We can talk."

What can we talk about?

Morning muddling matters most.

"Thank you." Paisley followed her into the cottage with the basket clutched in her arms. Cactus sniffed at her before going back to curl up in his blanket by the fire. "We still haven't heard from my mother. The police promised to look into her disappearance."

"And?"

"I've brought her planner from the office. Maybe you could take another look? See if you missed anything?" Paisley set the basket down on the table and pointed to the book underneath the tea. "I won't keep you. Please call me if you find anything."

Without giving Motts a chance to respond, Paisley spun around and practically jogged out of the cottage. Had there even been a point in inviting her inside? Had she really just dropped off a basket and run?

Motts followed her down the hall only to get a last glimpse of Paisley's vehicle reversing down the drive. "Maybe I'll have Dempsey taste test the scones first."

Setting the food to one side, Motts focused on the planner. She sat down at the kitchen table with Cactus stretched out beside her. They both peered down at the crisp handwriting that flowed across each page.

"I will never achieve this level of penmanship." Motts jolted in the chair when the doorbell rang. Again. "It can't be Paisley."

It wasn't.

Dempsey gave her the briefest wave before having to catch Cactus, who'd leapt up at him. "Hello to you too."

"No lunch?"

"Your twins insisted on bringing lunch by in an hour." Dempsey stepped into the cottage, ducking to avoid hitting his head on the doorframe. "They wanted to give us time to chat."

"Did they?" Motts shook her head with a tired sigh. She had no doubts the twins were trying to hook her up with Beck and considered Dempsey a contingency plan. And by the twins, she meant Vina. Nish had more sense. "Tea?"

"If you don't mind." He carried Cactus into the kitchen, taking a seat at the table. "How have you been?"

"You saw me last night." Motts busied herself, getting the kettle going and pulling down two mugs. "Not much happens in less than twenty-four hours."

"You'd be surprised."

Shrugging in response, Motts continued her hunt for an interesting tea blend before grabbing a tin of dark chocolate chai Vina's girlfriend had brought from India. Taara always gave interesting gifts, usually involving flavours they hadn't tried yet.

It smelled divine. The entire kitchen smelled of chocolate and spice. She let Dempsey entertain himself with Cactus, who thrived on the attention while she finished brewing tea.

"I've been fine." Motts carried two mugs over, setting one in front of him. "Why are you here?"

"Always straight to the point." He sniffed the tea appreciatively. "Nice. Not a blend I've tried before."

"Yes."

Dempsey chuckled. "I mentioned we've been tracking down the girls from your year at school."

"Yes," she repeated. She frowned into her steaming mug of tea. "And?"

"Is impatience why you prefer blunt honesty to dancing around the issue?"

Motts stared at his nose for a moment. "Teasing?"

"I'm indeed only teasing." Dempsey set his mug down. "We've managed to locate all but three of your classmates. Of the ones we've found, ten of the fifteen have either been reported missing or died under suspicious circumstances."

Motts sat heavily into a chair across from him. She set her mug down, sloshing tea over the rim. "What?"

Dempsey grabbed a tea towel off the chair next to him to mop up her tea. "The five we've found alive live outside of England. Two are in Australia, one in New Zealand, and the others are in the United States."

"Ten dead."

"Eleven if you count your friend Jenny." Dempsey reached out to grip her still trembling hand. "We're continuing to attempt to find the remaining three."

"Eleven." Motts didn't know how to process so many deaths. "A serial killer?"

"We don't have enough—" He cut himself off with a sharp shake of the head. "Blunt honesty time. In my educated opinion? Yes. Maybe not all the deaths are connected, but I don't believe in coincidences. I wanted you to be aware of the progress we've made so far."

Motts could only nod. She pulled her hand away and clutched her mug, trying to soak in the warmth. "Thank you."

"What's all this?" Dempsey gestured toward the open planner, trying to change the subject. "Someone's incredibly organised."

Motts hesitated for a second. She shifted her chair further around the table and dragged the planner over so they could both see it. "Someone's asked me to check into the disappearance of their mother."

"Have they?"

"Yes." Motts couldn't help her shoulders going

up a little. She was doing a fair imitation of Moss. "They did."

"Well?" Dempsey grabbed one of the scones, biting into it before continuing. "Where are we starting?"

"Pardon?"

"Fancy a tagalong while you investigate?" Dempsey continued to casually eat his scone. "I'm a dab hand at spotting clues."

"You... want to investigate with me?" Motts stared at the stubble on Dempsey's chin. She counted the grey in amongst the black hairs while trying to decipher if he was being facetious. *Is he not going to try to stop me?* "Aren't you supposed to be deterring me? Telling me to keep my nose out and leave this to the professionals."

"I'm technically off duty and on vacation. Cornwall isn't my jurisdiction." Dempsey sipped his tea and bent forward to inspect the planner. "Plus, I might learn something."

"From?"

"Your approach to mysteries." He tapped a finger against the right page of the planner. "She meticulously crossed off her to-do lists leading up to Thursday. When did she going missing?"

"Her daughter isn't sure. Or, she hasn't told me."

Motts didn't know how to take his easy acceptance of her trying to investigate Petunia's disappearance. "She said her mum's boyfriend claimed a note was left saying she'd gone on vacation."

"Left where?"

Motts dug underneath a stack of her origami paper to find a notebook. She wanted to write down a list of questions for Paisley before she forgot. "At her home, I assumed."

"Never assume." Dempsey raised his mug to salute her. "Have you been to her home?"

"Only her office."

"Well?" Dempsey drained the rest of his tea. "How about we finish checking out her planner then see if her daughter will let you snoop around her home?"

"Are you allowed to do that?"

"I'm merely observing the techniques of a private investigator." Dempsey winked at her. "Consider me nothing more than a benign shadow."

"I've mentioned this before, but do you actually inhale literature to rearrange the words and regurgitate them?" Motts mouthed the words "benign shadow" several times. She liked them. "Benignly bent backwards, breaching boredom."

"Nice alliteration."

The planner proved useless. One name, Ernest Herring, appeared most often on the days and times outside of work. Petunia had been a woman who organised every minute, even her time off and her dates with her boyfriend.

No clues leapt off the page to Motts.

"Why don't we have a tour of the brewery?"

"Saw the office already." Motts flipped through the pages of the planner one last time. "I'll text Paisley. Maybe we can get in one of the tours they run."

Dempsey glanced up from perusing a few notes Petunia had jotted down on the monthly page when the doorbell rang. "Lunch is served."

With a sigh of resignation, Motts made her way to the door. She hadn't seen Vina since her panic attack at the café. Her best friend was likely about to overtly demonstrate how sorry she was to have caused it.

Motts pulled the door open. "Vi—"

"Sorry." Vina didn't let her finish. "I pushed. I shouldn't have. And I'm sorry for making you uncomfortable."

"Vina."

Vina held out a large casserole dish. "Mum's best biryani. Friends?"

Motts shifted uneasily before reaching out to

awkwardly hug Vina with the casserole dish squashed between them. "Cactus missed his auntie Vina."

"Of course he did." Vina stepped back with a laugh. She lifted up the container again. "I brought food."

"Bribes buy back buddies." Motts gave Vina another quick hug. "Sorry I ignored your text."

"I brought Granny Martha's honey and apricot scones." River popped out behind Vina. "Forgive me too?"

"Fine. But only because you got Granny to make scones." Motts glanced over her shoulder to find Dempsey holding Cactus. She turned back to River and Vina, who were watching her intently. "We're investigating."

"We?" Vina raised her eyebrows.

"Shut up."

They made an uncomfortable quartet over a loud lunch. Motts was seconds away from ordering everyone out when River dragged Vina off. She followed them down the hall, ignoring their teasing.

Her cousin and best friend were nosy, noisy, and not funny. Motts was relieved when they left. Their energy had been too much for her.

"Finally." Motts closed the door on Vina and

River. She scowled at Dempsey when he chuckled. "You're not related to them."

"Is Pravina family?"

"Family is what you make of it. And I've made her—and the Griffins, in general—mine." She shrugged. "River's actual family, though."

"Do you need a break from people?" Dempsey placed Cactus on the table. "I've got several days here in Polperro. We can inspect the brewery tomorrow, and I can ask the rest of my questions."

Motts did suddenly have the urge to crawl into bed and hide for the rest of the day. "What questions?"

"They can wait," he assured her.

Another night of tossing and turning, wondering what he wants?

No thanks.

Going over to the kettle, Motts decided to make another mug of tea, this time a calming chamomile and lavender blend. She slowed her breathing, trying to count her inhales and exhales. *I can handle this.*

I can. No matter what the questions are. It's the only way we're ever going to find out what happened to Jenny.

While Motts stared at the electric kettle, Dempsey whispered to Cactus. He waited patiently for her, petting the loudly purring cat. Motts made a second mug of tea for him as well.

"What questions?" Motts asked once she'd made the tea. She sat at the table, clutching the mug to soak up some warmth. "About Jenny?"

"In a way. Mostly about your school." He accepted the tea and pulled a notebook out of his pocket. "Tell me about the adults—teachers, caretakers, anyone who was there frequently, who might've stood out to you. Kids often pick up on things."

Motts blinked at him a few times, trying to process. "I barely remember what I ate yesterday."

"Try. You might be surprised at what you recall."

With a frustrated groan, Motts cast her mind back to primary school. She hadn't been great with names, faces, or reading people's intentions then or now. No one really jumped out at her.

Unless....

"How old do you think the killer is now?" Motts had a vague recollection of most of the adults at her school, and they'd mostly been in their thirties or older. "Would they be in their sixties or seventies now?"

"Serial killers do age."

"Fair point." Motts still didn't have any idea. "Wait. Creepy smoker."

"Who?"

"Spotty-faced teenager who chain-smoked on the corner, waiting for his little brother, who I think was in our year or the one above." Motts had the vaguest memory of the two. "No clue what their surname was. They lived near the school. Jonty and Hugo, maybe? Jonty was the younger, probably short for Jonathan. I never heard anyone call him anything other than Jonty."

"Can you remember anything else about them?" Dempsey asked after making a few notes.

"Mum might." Motts shook her head after thinking for a few minutes. "Think she knew their parents."

"Why was Hugo creepy?"

"He used to make comments about us, whispering when he thought we couldn't hear him." Motts had a sudden recollection of Jenny telling their teacher about Hugo. She had a flood of half-memories, almost like photos with parts cut out. "I don't think I saw him again after Jenny's death, but I can't be sure."

Dempsey continued to jot down in his notebook before finally returning it to his pocket. "Why don't you relax for the rest of the day? I want to make a few calls and get my team out to see who Jonty and

Hugo are. We can traipse around the brewery tomorrow."

Traipse.

"Traipse. Traipse. I want to make an alliteration, but it's too good on its own." Motts enjoyed the feel of the word. "Why are you here?"

"Vacation."

"I don't believe you." Motts thought Dempsey had what her uncle Tom would call a good poker face. "Never mind."

"I'll see you in the morning." Dempsey let himself out of the cottage, leaving Motts to consider enigmatic detective inspectors with remarkable vocabularies.

"Eloquent efficient. Why doesn't his name start with E? It would be so convenient." Motts turned to Cactus, who stretched his paws out toward her. "Yes, I agree. Why didn't he simply email his questions to me from London? Surely those didn't require a five- or six-hour trek out to Polperro?"

CHAPTER SEVEN

"I brought you a gift." Dempsey held out a hard black case. "I've followed a few autistic vloggers. They swear by these Bose noise-cancelling headphones."

"Vloggers?"

Dempsey handed over the case then took a sip of his coffee. "I enjoy listening to them when I'm driving to work. Are you planning to give me a lift on your scooter?"

"You wouldn't fit." Motts eyed him up for a moment. "You were joking."

"I was. And I'll drive. We wouldn't want to show up dishevelled from a wild Vespa ride along the coast." Dempsey had another drink of coffee. "Shall we?"

Motts lifted up the new headphones. "Why?"

"I thought perhaps being able to simply cut off all the noise from the world might allow you more freedom." He tossed his keys up into the air a few times. "And you don't have to deafen yourself by turning the volume up higher and higher."

The headphones were a thoughtful gift. Motts didn't know what to make of it. She stood there clutching the box for almost a full minute without speaking.

"Motts?"

She quit staring at the zipper on the case and gave a jerky nod. "Thank you."

Dempsey waved off her thanks. He swiftly changed the subject, much to her relief. "I made a few calls last night. We haven't found Hugo and Jonty. I've got a few detectives following up with the school in the hopes of getting more information."

"Okay." Motts felt as though the gift had pressed pause on her brain. She tried to get things back on track. "Right. Paisley offered to give us a tour of the brewery this morning. I said you were a friend who also did investigations."

"Not an inaccurate statement. Why don't you try out the headphones on the drive to the brewery?" Dempsey suggested.

Noise-cancelling headphones, Motts discovered, were quite possibly the greatest invention in the world. She'd tried a few types of earbuds over the years. None of them had been quite so effective.

There were clouds over her ears.

Cushiony, cosy, comforting clouds.

Blissfully silent ones.

Motts sat on the drive to Looe, flicking the noise-cancelling switch on and off. She stopped when Dempsey began to chuckle. "These are brilliant."

"I'm glad." Dempsey deftly squeezed his Range Rover into a space in the parking lot. "Shall we?"

Motts didn't want to leave the blissful muffled world of her new headphones. She reluctantly returned them to the case. "Thanks for the gift of peace."

Before Dempsey could reply, Paisley came rushing out of the building. She seemed incredibly excited to see them. An odd emotion given the circumstances, or so Motts thought.

She had a distinct feeling Paisley wasn't comfortable in her own skin. She kept changing styles and mannerisms with the new clothes. Today she was brightly dressed and overly animated. "Hello."

Hello?

Could I make one word sound even more awkward?

Note to self: don't take that as a challenge.

"The tour starts in an hour. Thought you and your friend might enjoy experiencing a proper one. Give you an idea of what Mum did here." Paisley motioned for them to follow her inside. "You can look around until it starts. I'm filling in for Mum for a bit."

Are you now?

Interesting.

Once again, in the narrow passage running along the right side of the warehouse, Motts felt a shiver of apprehension. The brewery gave off strange vibes. It creeped her out.

She'd been in the Chen-Mottley brewery hundreds of times. It had never once affected her. She couldn't help wondering if something terrible had happened to Petunia Lee.

Don't overreact.

Maybe I should catch up with Dempsey.

The detective inspector had made his way into the brewhouse, and Motts decided to follow. Her inspection thus far hadn't revealed anything useful. He might see something she hadn't.

"Everything okay?" Dempsey stood in front of a

row of barrels. He frowned when she raced up but accepted her muttered assurances. "What do you see?"

"Barrels."

"Aside from the obvious."

Motts glanced at each of the barrels. She noticed the front of them contained a series of numbers plus a date. A second look at the row revealed one discrepancy. "There's one missing."

Each barrel had an individual number. They appeared to run sequentially, which made sense. One was definitely gone from the middle of the lot.

Dempsey nodded his agreement. He pointed toward the second row of casks behind them. "All the other rows are complete."

"Petunia likes to be organised." Motts recalled the meticulous nature of the woman's planner. "If you were a missing cask, where would you be?"

"Outside."

Motts immediately went to peer out the window. It offered a great view of the rest of the property. "My guess would be the run-down shed in the distant pasture. Or, if I'm being pedantic, it's probably a barn, not a shed."

"Are you often pedantic with yourself? Don't answer." Dempsey smiled at her. He came over to stand behind her, looking out the window. "Why there?"

She decided he was genuinely interested in her thought process. "Shed's old. Damaged. I imagine part of the original farm. And no one would have a reason to go out there."

Since they had over thirty minutes until the tour started, they snuck out the side exit. Motts's sense of trepidation grew with each step. She couldn't shake the dread settling on her chest.

They'd just reached the shed when Paisley came racing up to them. She gave Dempsey permission to open the door when he asked. Motts wondered if she'd been keeping an eye on them.

"Have you found anything?" Paisley asked.

"We don't know yet." Dempsey managed to get the wooden door open, leaning it against the wall. "I think you should both stay outside for a moment."

Motts hadn't intended to go into the manky old shed. Paisley had other ideas. She shoved into her, forcing both of them into the dusty, dimly lit space. "What the devil is that smell? Smells like death pickles. Pickles and soilage."

The barn had definitely seen better days. It looked as though someone had simply shoved every leftover piece of farm equipment from the last century into the building. Motts was momentarily distracted by dust floating in the air.

Focus.

"Brine," Paisley interjected. "Smells like the mixture used to make pickles."

"I'd like you two to step outside." Dempsey stood beside a barrel partially hidden behind a stack of old wooden crates.

"What is it?" Paisley stumbled forward. Her elbow caught Motts in the back, sending her flying. "Sorry."

Motts tripped over a length of rope, stumbled past Dempsey into the barrel. Her arm pushed off the lid, and she recoiled immediately at the sight of a hand sticking out of the murky liquid. "Oh, holy mother of mittens."

"Outside. Now." Dempsey firmly yet gently forced them out of the shed when Paisley peered into the barrel and began to scream. He kept his arm around Motts, keeping her on her feet. He grabbed his phone once outside and placed a call. "Inspector Ash? We've found a body."

"Mum was pickled." Paisley stopped screaming long enough to get the words out.

Motts covered her face with her hands, trying not to sick up her breakfast. She regretted not having her new headphones and also had to smother an entirely inappropriate desire to laugh at Paisley's statement. "I'd really hoped to be over this trend of finding dead bodies. Welcome to Cornwall. Death is right around the corner."

AFTER TWO COLD CASE INVESTIGATIONS, MOTTS was immune to the calm chaos of a crime scene. Paisley had fainted not long after the police arrived. Paramedics had carted her off to an ambulance for observation.

It was a bit dramatic. She hadn't swooned at the sight of her mum in a barrel; why do so now? Motts didn't know what to make of her.

Finding a clear spot in the grass a safe ways from the shed, Motts had sat down to watch the police work. *They should reword the quote about curiosity killing the cat. All it seems to do is bring me dead bodies.*

"Thought you might appreciate these." Dempsey

crouched in front of her and held out the headphone case. "Are you doing all right?"

"Better than Petunia." Motts held the case loosely in her hands. "Was she pickled to death?"

Dempsey cleared his throat several times, making Motts peer up at him. "I doubt it. The killer likely thought brine would kill the smell of decomposing flesh."

"I could've gone my entire life without hearing someone utter those words all together in a sentence." Motts groaned. She tried desperately not to think about what had been in the barrel. "Don't think I'll ever eat another pickle."

Dempsey coughed repeatedly.

"Are you coming down with a cold?"

"No."

"Is laughing one of those weird police coping mechanisms?" Motts tried to remember the phrase she'd heard in a documentary. "Dark humour?"

"I suppose there is a hint of the macabre," he acknowledged. "We all deal with things as we can. You do seem to stumble on the most unique cases."

Motts shrugged. She eased the headphones out of the case and put them on. They were amazingly brilliant at muffling the myriad of sounds she couldn't tune out.

"Why don't I give you a lift home? They'll be combing through the entire property for most of the day. We'll be in the way." Dempsey stood up, rubbing his knee with a painful groan. "They know where to find you if they have questions."

"Inspector Ash won't appreciate my interference. He's particular." Motts had found a great friend in Marnie Ash; her husband could be a little intimidating at times. "I wonder how Petunia died."

Taking one last glance across the pasture, Motts spotted something glinting in the distance. She ignored Dempsey and strode across the grass to the stone wall around the property. A pair of binoculars was resting on the top of it.

"Odd." Motts leaned up on her toes to get a better view. "One of the lenses is smashed. I'd wager they dropped these. Why leave them here?"

"Don't touch them. I imagine the detectives will want to check for prints." Dempsey led her across the pasture to where the detectives were waiting. "We're off for Polperro."

"Hello, Motts. Fancy seeing you here." Hughie waved from behind the two detectives. "Have you met Detective Inspector Yuen?"

Motts waved at the lovely police officer. She could see why Hughie had a crush on the woman.

Don't be awkward. Say hello. "Pineapple Mottley. Everyone calls me Motts."

Not everyone. Most people. She doesn't need to know that.

"You live up in Daisy's old cottage. Rebecca Yuen." She held her hand out.

Motts stared at the hand a few seconds before reaching out to shake it. "Hughie said some excellent things about you."

Hughie glared at her over the heads of the detectives. "Nice things."

"I said nice. Well, excellent, same difference," Motts argued.

"This is lovely, but we should go." Dempsey finished his whispered conversation with Percy and pulled Motts away from them. He was quiet until they'd gotten to his vehicle. "Hughie's gone an interesting shade of pink."

"River would call him a bear." Motts noticed a burly man, in his fifties, standing near the entrance to the warehouse, arguing with a younger man. She recognised the latter from a photo Paisley had shown her of her boyfriend. "Wonder who he is?"

"Heath Miller. He's the current brewmaster." Dempsey unlocked the vehicle and got inside. "I listened in while they questioned him."

"They let you?" Motts fumbled with the seat belt before finally getting it across her body. "Because you're a detective?"

"Because they didn't notice I was listening." Dempsey winked at her when she rolled her eyes. "I've got years on those three. You'd be amazed at how quickly people forget you when you're simply leaning against a wall not interacting."

"I wouldn't be amazed." Motts tapped her fingers against the headphone case. "Not if you were quiet. People ignore you then."

And they did.

"Nothing wrong with being quiet." Dempsey kept his attention on the manoeuvring around midmorning traffic.

Motts had an entire life's worth of experience with people forgetting she existed. Quiet, in her opinion, was often underrated by neurotypicals. "Did you learn anything about Heath Miller?"

"He's not a fan of Petunia."

Motts was genuinely surprised Dempsey had willingly shared anything with her. The other detective inspectors in her life had gone out of their way to deter her from getting involved. "Oh?"

"To paraphrase, he wasn't sorry to see her gone." Dempsey took a left, taking the road leading down to

Talland Bay. "Mind if we have a detour? I am on vacation after all."

"Are you?" Motts still felt suspicious at his need to come all the way to Cornwall to ask a few questions. Her curiosity about Heath won out for the moment. "Did Heath say anything else?"

"About?" Dempsey held a hand up when she went to complain. "He resented Petunia and Paisley for their presence at the brewery. Make of that what you will. He felt he should have the run of the place. Didn't mince words about their ruining a grand tradition. I also overheard the brewery has limited CCTV cameras inside the warehouse and focusing on the car park but none in the office or on the rest of the property."

Finding the beach relatively empty, Dempsey eased into a parking space. He twisted in his seat towards Motts. She narrowed her eyes suspiciously on him.

Is he going to explain why he drove all the way to Polperro to ask questions?

Probably not.

"You could ask me the question on your mind." Dempsey pulled his keys out of the ignition and pocketed them. "The anticipation is distracting."

Motts fidgeted with the seat belt. The buckle seemed intensely fascinating. "Pardon?"

"Just ask."

She continued toying with the seat belt. She eventually clicked the buckle in when Dempsey reached out to take it out of her hands. "Why are you here?"

"Taking you home after driving you to a crime scene?"

"And people accuse me of being pedantic." She wasn't immune to the power of his easy-going smile. She had no doubts his ability to be disarming helped him in interrogations. "Emailing your questions would've been a whole lot simpler than driving all the way to Cornwall."

"Maybe I wanted to see Cactus."

"Maybe you're full of bollocks." Motts decided since she had neither his charm nor his impressive glare, she'd settle for frowning at his chin. "You know what I meant. Stop snickering. I...."

Trailing off into silence, Motts found it hard to express her thoughts. She stared out at the sea, searching for words. Dempsey waited patiently beside her.

She appreciated it.

"Is this a sex thing? I don't do that." Motts wrinkled her nose. She shuddered. "Gross. I mean, not you. You're brilliant, I'm sure. I'll shut up now. Bugger."

Dempsey snorted in amusement and laughed for almost two minutes. "No, nothing to do with sex. Why would you even think that?"

"Experience with not understanding neurotypicals. Nine times out of ten, it's sex." Motts scratched her head absently. She felt the sudden urge to apologise for assuming. "Sorry?"

Dempsey shook his head, still chuckling. "Safe assumption to make, I suppose. Why don't we walk on the beach before those storm clouds decide to open up?"

"Fine."

Talland Bay was one of Motts's favourite spots outside of Looe. The beach was beautiful. She loved the ice cream shop nearby as well.

Grey clouds had completely blocked out the sun. Motts loved the scent of rain mixed with the sea air. She picked up a seashell on her way down toward the shoreline.

Waves crashing on the sand soothed the edges of stress building from the chaotic morning. The ocean always managed to carry away her frustration. Her shoulders lowered within minutes.

Motts glanced around, spotting Dempsey sitting on a boulder watching her. She made her way slowly across the beach to him. "You think the killer hasn't finished."

Dempsey patted the rock, motioning for her to join him. "I don't believe the disappearances and murders of almost an entire year from the same school is a coincidence."

Motts jumped up onto the boulder. "And I'd be on the list."

"You're remarkably perceptive."

"You're worried I'm next." Motts stared out at the crashing waves. "Maybe not next, but the list is incredibly short at this point."

"Whoever the killer is, they're persistent. It's been years. They're still focusing on their target." He considered his next words for a few seconds. "The most recent death was two years ago."

Motts pulled her legs up and rested her chin on her knees. "Jenny and I always walked home from school together."

"You mentioned."

"Maybe the killer thought they'd get a two-for-one deal." She ran her finger over the grooves of the shell. "How worried should I be?"

The question wasn't the one she wanted to ask.

The words had stuck in her throat. She didn't have the courage to ask if a serial killer might be stalking her.

Am I next?

Did he save me for last?

Or, she?

Or, they?

Who knows... am I going to be the next mystery to be solved?

Despite the calm presence of the sea, Motts found her thoughts racing chaotically. Moments from school began to flash through her mind. She couldn't stop the steady stream of potential suspects from scrolling.

"Let's get you home." Dempsey's voice jolted her out of her thoughts. She'd forgotten he was there. "You're going into shock. Your version of it."

Helping her off the boulder, Dempsey guided her off the beach to his vehicle. He grabbed a blanket from the boot and covered her. Motts hadn't realised her whole body had begun to shake.

Wrapped in the fleece, Motts took the head-phones Dempsey handed to her and sank into the warm solitude. He spent a few minutes on his phone before putting the car in drive.

In the quiet, Motts didn't hear much over the

fuzziness in her head. She hid behind the blanket. Dempsey seemed content to drive in silence.

"Motts?" Dempsey waved a hand in front of her face. "Cactus awaits your presence."

It took a few seconds for Motts to extract herself from the blanket and force herself to get out of the vehicle. Drizzling rain and a mild breeze off the sea hit her almost immediately. She breathed in deeply, tilting her head back to let the raindrops caress her face.

"There's magic up here." Dempsey waited patiently for her to finish breathing in the sea.

"The best decision I ever made was moving from London out here." Motts fished out her keys and opened her front door. Cactus immediately brushed by her to see Dempsey. "I see where your priorities are."

Meow.

"Yes, yes, he's new." Motts set the headphone case on the counter. She didn't know what to do with herself. "You'll change your tune when you want flaky tuna later."

"Don't forget to lock the door." Dempsey gave Cactus one last scratch. "Lunch will be soon."

He'd been gone over ten minutes before Motts moved from standing by the door. She glanced out the window to the right of the door, spotting her cousin and Nish coming up the path. They were obviously bringing the lunch Dempsey mentioned.

"Amma made curry shepherd's pie last night." Nish lifted the covered dish in his hands. "Vina's managing the café. She'll be by later with supper for you."

"I made the heroic gesture of braving Innis for a bucket of chips." River had a bag in one hand and a Tupperware container in the other. "Mum made pineapple jam tarts for you. See? It's you in a dessert."

Motts sent her cousin a withering glare. He grinned in response. "You have a bag, not a bucket. Should you both be at work?"

"Dempsey sent a text about you having a rough morning. Dad gave me the day off. You're welcome." River shifted the bag into his other hand then lifted his arm. "Hug?"

"Chips." Motts grabbed the bag from the Salty Seaman. "Hugs later."

"Fair enough."

While River entertained Cactus, Motts and Nish spread the food dishes out on the coffee table. They got plates and silverware from the kitchen. She curled up in her armchair with her lunch, which mainly consisted of a massive pile of chips.

Nish went over to get the fire going, having noticed her shivering. "Do you want to tell us what happened?"

Motts shook her head. She shoved her shepherd's pie around with a fork. "Not now."

CHAPTER NINE

The following morning, the sun was out, and Motts decided to clear her mind. A ramble around the coast sounded brilliant. She'd wanted to visit the Rame Head; now seemed the perfect time.

She cycled into the village to grab a few treats for the trip. Vina greeted her cheerfully from the counter of Griffin Brews. Nish popped out of the kitchen with a large baking tray. "Hello, twins."

"Morning, fruity one." Nish carefully balanced the tray while Vina moved the croissants into a basket. "Where are you off to?"

"Cremyll. Or maybe just Rame Head." Motts eased her thermos out and set it on the counter. "Can I get some tea?"

"Want company on your walk?" Vina asked with zero enthusiasm. "Here. We've got cheddar and chutney sandwiches with the crusts cut off, so you can't whine about them. Amma made her tomato chutney for this. Almost like having a grilled cheese and tomato soup. I'll throw in two curry chocolate pasties and maybe a couple of macarons for you."

"Brilliant. Thanks. Also, you hate long walks and cycling. It's going to take me two hours to get to the start of the walking path." Motts began packing the bags Vina offered to her in the food section of her backpack. She slotted the thermos in the netting on the other side. "I'll be back this afternoon."

"Be careful." Nish held out a mini breakfast quiche. "Sure you don't want company? I'm not bad on a long bike trip."

Leaving the twins to argue over who was the least or most athletic, Motts ate her quiche while heading out to her bike. She secured her backpack in the basket at the front. It was tempting to ride her Vespa instead, but the peace of a cycling trip won out.

At a moderate pace, Motts managed to make the car park at the end of Ramehead Lane in two hours. She found a safe place to lock up her bike. Taking a sip of water, she secured the bottle, then slipped on her backpack.

Let's find somewhere to have a snack.

The two-hour cycle had left her wanting something to eat. Motts strolled from the car park down the coastal path, veering off toward St Michael's Chapel. She climbed up the hill, pausing to enjoy the views on either side, then around the old stone church to sit on the ledge at the back.

Pale blue skies met the deeper blue sea. She grabbed an extra jumper out of the bag and tugged it over her head. A wicked breeze was battering the church on the hill and her with it.

Half a thermos of tea and a sandwich later, Motts was ready for a ramble. She walked back up the path and continued on the circuit. The dry brush danced in the wind as she went by.

Autumn had turned the hills a mixture of brown and green. Hints of fire-coloured leaves mingled in here and there. She kept her gaze on the well-travelled dirt path; she didn't want to take a tumble over the cliff.

She hadn't slept the greatest the previous night. Her mind hadn't settled despite her best efforts. True crime wasn't quite so fascinating when the killer might be after her.

I can't do anything about a potential killer who may or may not be hunting me.

The only thing I can do is panic.

I'm brilliant at panicking.

In parts the hedge had grown high enough to block her view, but finally Motts came out into the more open pasture. Horses grazed. She paused for several minutes to have a chat with them.

I should've brought sugar cubes for them.

Continuing on down the path, Motts found the sign she'd been looking for. She went up a hill to explore the Queen's grotto. It scared her a little with the cold wind whipping through, so she returned to the path.

After walking for an hour, Motts already felt better. She had no control over what anyone else did. Stressing over possibilities would do nothing but increase her blood pressure.

And it was high enough without panicking over a serial killer.

Deciding to leave exploring St Andrew's Church for another day, Motts went through Caws and continued on the path. She considered stopping in the village for lunch but decided to hold off. It would be better to finish up the circuit, then eat.

When Motts arrived at the car park, she found

her uncle Tom waiting for her. He opened the back of the brewery delivery van and helped her lift her bicycle into it. She wondered who'd called him.

"Enjoy your walk, young Pineapple?" He sat on the rear bumper while she fished out her water bottle for a drink. "Had lunch yet?"

"Had a few sandwiches earlier." Motts still had a few pasties and macarons in her backpack. "I could stand to eat, though. Were you making a delivery in Plymouth?"

"I was earlier. Nish texted me. It's pouring down rain in Polperro. He didn't want you to get stuck out." He nodded toward the clouds building up in the distance. "Fancy a bap from the Copley Arms? It should be open by the time we're near Hessenford."

"Sure." Motts could do with their halloumi fries with chilli jam.

The drive from Rame Head to Hessenford went by quickly. Motts listened to her uncle chatter about his day. She made sure to nod in all the appropriate places while enjoying the warmth of the van.

"What's got you so worried?" her uncle asked once they'd picked up lunch at the pub and driven down to Seaton Beach. "Did that detective inspector from London upset you? Does he need a good talking to?"

"Uncle Tomato." Motts had to chuckle at the mental image of him lecturing Dempsey. "Detective Inspector Byrne is a nice bloke."

"A nice bloke?"

"He is," she muttered defensively. She picked at her halloumi fries while watching a couple walking their rambunctious dogs on the beach. "He's been working on Jenny's case."

Her uncle tensed immediately. "And?"

"They're still investigating." Motts gazed down at the plate of food in her lap. "The killer might still be active."

"Might?"

Motts shrugged. What else could she say? Dempsey hadn't exactly had many details to share.

"You be careful, young Pineapple. I know you're all alone up on the hill." He reached over to squeeze her shoulder gently. "Keep your security system on at all times."

Shrugging once again, Motts focused on her chips and the dogs frolicking on the beach. They chased each other around, then dashed off down the sand. The two appeared to be playing a game with the waves, darting toward them then racing away just in time to avoid getting soaked.

"You knew Petunia Lee, right?" Motts decided a

change of subject was in order. "Who do you think killed her?"

"Motts."

"Uncle."

"Your auntie would know more than me." He sipped his tea slowly. "Petunia had a fantastic row with her daughter's boyfriend. I can't remember his name. His parents own the brewery."

"Louis Banks."

"That's the one." He pointed his cup at her.

"Do you know what the row was about?" Motts was intrigued since Paisley hadn't mentioned an argument. "When did this happen?"

"Maybe a few weeks ago? Or perhaps about a week before Petunia went missing." He finished up the last of his bap and shoved the wrapper in a bag. "They were rowing about their ale recipe. Petunia refused to change, while Louis wanted to try out trendier flavours."

"Trendier?"

"Dirty four-letter word."

"Except, it's more than four?" Motts pointed out. "What's a 'trendy' flavour?"

"Cotton candy?"

"Cotton candy ale?" Motts felt mildly queasy. "Can you remember anything else?"

"You'll have to ask your auntie. She was there for it." He finished up his last bit of tea. "Ready?"

With their lunch and her interrogation finished, he drove her home and right into the rain. They got her bicycle in the shed, and she dashed into the cottage. Cactus watched her from his bed, barely lifting his head up.

"And how was your day? Lazy cat." Motts emptied her backpack, leaving both her thermos and water bottle in the sink to clean later. Cactus followed her into the kitchen. "Yes, I'm aware you've missed out on your afternoon snack."

Meow.

"Have I treated you terribly? Is it a fish or a cheese type of offence?" Motts filled his dish with a snack and carried it into the living room for him. She got a fire going, then sank down into her armchair with a tired groan. "Clearing one's mind is an exhausting exercise."

After a while, Motts went upstairs to run a bath. The cycle and walk had been good for her mind. Her body wasn't quite so sure about it.

While lazing in the warm bath, Motts considered what her uncle had said. Paisley and Louis definitely had questions to answer. She wasn't sure asking them directly would be the best idea.

Meow.

Motts leaned up to find Cactus sitting on the bathroom rug. "Ready for another snack?"

CHAPTER TEN

THE FOLLOWING MORNING, MOTTS WOKE UP with a desire to forget about serial killers. She focused instead on Petunia. It was a mystery that seemed easier to solve and less frightening.

Mikey was helping Callie and Lillith, who owned and ran the kayak shop in Fowey. Motts decided to pay them a visit. She might learn more about Paisley.

After spending time with Cactus in the garden having breakfast, Motts headed out on her Vespa. She arrived in time to grab the ferry across to Fowey. The forty-minute ride had gone by quickly; traffic had diminished with fewer tourists.

Callie's Kayaks wasn't open when Motts arrived. She parked her Vespa, then popped by Brown Sugar

Café for a warm mug of tea and several teacakes with blackberry jam. Going down Market Street, she found a bench to sit on and eat a late breakfast.

"Motts!"

Motts swallowed her last bite of teacake and twisted around to find a cheerful Mikey waving at her. "Hello."

Getting up, Motts wiped her hands on a napkin. She dropped it in a nearby rubbish bin. Mikey attempted a hug but pulled back when she held him off with her tea.

"What brings you to Fowey?" He waited for her to gather herself. "Just wanted tea and cake?"

"Came to see Callie and you, actually." Motts walked down the street, Mikey easily falling in step with her. "How's Ashby?"

Both Ashby and Mikey had been suspects in the murder of the latter's grandmother, Nadine O'Connell. Somehow, they'd gone from being involved in a criminal investigation to boyfriends. They were a cute couple.

"He's walking in Wales for a month. Have you seen his Instagram?" Mikey asked. He peered down at her after a moment. "What questions did you have?"

"Paisley."

"Ahh."

"Yes, ahh. Can you tell me about Paisley and Louis? Do you know both of them?" Motts rested her tea on a window ledge while searching in her backpack for a notebook and pen. "I wrote down my questions."

"How very organised," Mikey teased. He waved to someone across the street then guided Motts down the pavement. "Why don't we talk in the shop? I promised Callie that I'd open up for her."

"Are you not running a warehouse in Polperro?" Motts hadn't heard any village gossip about the O'Connell family business. The fishermen would've been quite vocal about losing the icehouse. "I haven't seen you in a few weeks."

"Hired someone to run the warehouse for me." Mikey dug around in his pocket then pulled out a large set of keys. "It was too hard. Living and working in Polperro. I kept expecting my mum to come into the house screaming at Jasper or me to show up for work. I won't throw away everything my nan and granddad worked for, though."

"Probably wise." Motts couldn't imagine the trauma of dealing with two murdered relatives and an incarcerated brother. She wasn't surprised living in Polperro had soured for Mikey. "Glad you've found a community here in Fowey. Commune candidly coming cordially."

"Four Cs. Nice." Mikey opened the door to Callie's Kayaks. "So, what did you want to ask me about?"

"Paisley and Louis." Motts followed him into the shop. She waited by the door for him to turn the lights on and then sat on the couch in the back corner. "About their relationship together and with her mum. How do you know them?"

"Okay." Mikey began setting up the shop for the day. "Jasper and Louis played on opposing teams in the local footie club. We used to go out for pints afterwards."

"Right."

"Paisley and her mum were trying to rebuild their relationship. It's why she was so worried when her mum didn't respond. Or, so I assume from her texts." Mikey paused in raising the inner shutters on the windows. "Louis always claimed to be friendly with his future mother-in-law."

"But?"

Mikey crossed his arms, glancing out at a passing vehicle. "Louis was itching to run the brewery how he wanted. Family legacy and all that nonsense. I more than understood his perspective. He got on quite well with the other manager at the brewery—Heath or Henry. Maybe it was Harry?"

"Heath Miller?" Motts checked her notebook where she'd jotted down the names of several of the brewery employees. "My uncle said Petunia and Louis had a row over her management style."

"Management style?" Mikey snickered. He shook his head and let his arms fall to his side. "She was rigid in wanting to keep on a schedule. She refused to make changes. In fairness, I heard this from Louis, who'd drunk a fair bit and had a healthy grudge at her running of his family's brewery."

"How big of a grudge?" Motts pressed after he fell silent.

Mikey came over to sit beside her. "I don't know, Motts. Could he kill? I can't say. I never believed my mum or brother were capable of taking a life. And yet, they proved to be more than able to murder."

Motts patted his arm awkwardly, trying to offer some semblance of comfort. "Sorry. I shouldn't have asked."

"Not your fault," Mikey assured her. "A year ago, I would've said a firm no. Now? I'm not sure."

They sat in silence for a few minutes. Motts jotted down a few thoughts based on Mikey's responses. She didn't want to press him for more when he was obviously still healing.

"'ello, 'ello." Callie bounded into the shop with her wife, Lillith, close behind. "Morning, Motts. Fancy seeing you here. Doing another investigation?"

"Doing another investigation?" Lillith snorted in amusement at her wife. "How do you do an investigation?"

"Carefully, with a lot of questions?"

Deciding Mikey didn't have any additional information to offer, Motts left the trio to tease each other and open the shop. She'd done enough for one morning. Now she had to figure out how to approach Paisley and Louis.

At the top of her list, Motts wondered where Louis had been in the last week. Paisley had mentioned him being at university. Had he actually been there when Petunia went missing?

It shouldn't be too hard to find out.

After a quick stop in one of the local shops for a few jars of lemon curd, Motts made the drive back to Polperro. She decided to pop by Marnie's bridal shop. Marnie was always an excellent source of local gossip.

Plus, Marnie could occasionally be convinced to share the information she'd overheard from Perry.

"Hello, love." Marnie greeted when Motts pushed open the bridal shop door an hour later. "What brings you here? More bouquets? Or perhaps something a little more macabre?"

Motts decided since subtlety wasn't her strength, she might as well not bother. "Have you heard anything about Petunia's death? Or the brewery in Looe?"

"I knew you couldn't resist a new mystery. Heard Paisley asked you to investigate her mother's disappearance. Well, her murder, I suppose." Marnie finished draping a veil on one of her displays. "My Perry did mention you found the body. You've the worst luck of anyone I know."

"I'm aware." Motts didn't appreciate her new-found talent at finding the dead. She readily accepted a handful of chocolate buttons when Marnie held a bowl out to her. "So? Any pertinent gossip to share?"

"Me? Of course I do." Marnie waved her behind the counter. "Vina brought a few slices of a spiced coffee cake. Want to share with me?"

"Sugar and gossip."

"The basis of any good friendship." Marnie

offered her a little saucer with a slice of cake. "I can't tell you much. Perry's been quite quiet on the subject. I do know Paisley and Petunia put on a good show of being close in the last year."

"But?"

Marnie finished up her bite of cake. "Judi, who runs the Looe post office, claims the two were in a month ago, picking at each other over the silliest things. Petunia was a sweet woman. Sweet yet complicated. None of us are nice all the time. We all have rough days and quirks that might annoy someone else."

"No one's described her as sweet so far."

"Mostly sweet on occasion." Marnie wiped crumbs off the counter. "I did hear another juicy bit of gossip for you. Petunia and her boyfriend were hunting for an engagement ring. They visited a shop run by a friend of mine."

"Petunia? Not Paisley?" Motts was surprised.

"Yes, Petunia. They were supposed to pick the ring up last week." Marnie leaned in closer as if sharing a secret. "My friend said they never showed up at her shop. And, the following day, they'd cancelled the payment via their credit card company."

"Odd."

"Distinctly." Marnie nodded.

Before Motts could ask another question, one of the bridal shop clients came in for an appointment. She headed out, promising to keep Marnie updated. The gossip had given her plenty to think about.

Is it too early for lunch?

I'm going to need sustenance to sort through all my thoughts.

Deciding to give the Ferris Wheel a try, Motts rode her Vespa down the street and around the corner. She parked near the bistro and walked toward it. Beckett stood outside, writing out a menu on the chalkboard by the door.

"Fancy a brie, bacon, and cranberry panini? I'm about to make one for myself with some cheddar chips." Beckett finished up the menu and brushed their chalky hands off on their apron. "Bread is fresh from Griffin Brews. They're supplying loaves for me each day. Brilliant bakers over there."

Motts preened with pride over her best friends. "They are brilliant."

"They are."

"The panini sounds delicious." Motts followed them into the bistro. "What are cheese chips?"

"We double fry our potatoes, then cover them in a thick, creamy cheddar sauce," Beckett added an odd inflexion to the words "thick" and "creamy." Motts frowned, trying to figure out what the tone of voice meant. "You'll love them. Delicious."

"Are those your favourite words? Thick and creamy?" Motts asked, genuinely curious. The choked sound from Beckett told her that she'd missed something. "Right."

"Right."

"Flirting." Motts closed her eyes, counting to ten and breathing deeply. She opened them to find a bemused Beckett watching. "Or not? Probably not. Maybe you like those words. They're good ones. Foodie ones. I'm going to stop talking now."

Beckett's smile widened further. "They are good words. And we'll see about the flirting. First, though, sandwiches and chips."

Thankfully for Motts, Beckett seemed to understand how embarrassed she felt. They got her sandwich and chips placed in a to-go box. She fled home where it was safe—and she couldn't embarrass herself any further.

When Motts arrived at the cottage, she found a box with a note from Dempsey waiting for her. Gathering it up with her food and bag from the shop in Fowey, Motts managed to get inside without dropping anything. She set everything on the table and cuddled with Cactus while reading the note.

Meow.

"Yes, I was gone far too long. How did you survive?" Motts tried to read the message while Cactus continually head-butted her chin. "Shall I read the note to you? Or summarise? Dempsey's on his way to London. He's left a gift for you. Clever man."

After going back to lock the door, Motts peeked into the box. Dempsey had gifted her one of his detective notebooks and a rain poncho specifically for when she went on walks and cycling. She grinned at the catnip toy at the bottom.

Meow.

"Yes, I will make up lunch for you." Motts set him on the blanket on one side of the table. He immediately tried to grab the catnip stuffed toy. "Addict."

———

CHAPTER ELEVEN

"WHAT IS WRONG WITH MY NEPHEW?" VINA watched Cactus wriggle around on the hearth rug with a toy clutched between his paws. She'd come up to the cottage for a quiet dinner; Nish and River had gone to Fowey for a double date with Callie and Lillith. "Has he gotten catnip again? Poor little addict."

"Dempsey left a present before he returned to London." Motts steeled herself for the inevitable reaction. Vina immediately twisted around to stare at her. "Don't start."

"Pressies. He left pressies?" Vina leaned against the kitchen counter. She stared intently at her. "Tell me more."

"There was a box at my door when I came home

this afternoon." Motts didn't think the story required further details. "Why are you grinning like the Cheshire cat?"

"I keep telling you—"

"Dempsey's being friendly. Friends give gifts." Motts focused on dishing up the crispy salt and vinegar roasted potatoes and garlic chicken. "Your mum has outdone herself."

"I could've made this."

"You could've," Motts agreed readily. All of the Griffins were excellent chefs. "Still, your mum's the only one who crisps up roast potatoes like this."

"Rude, but true." Vina grabbed one of the plates, snagging one of the cloth napkins as well. "Mottsy?"

Motts glanced up from where she'd been attempting to put the perfect amount of ketchup on her plate. "What?"

"I am sorry, you know?"

"No, I don't." She didn't think Vina had done anything recently requiring an apology. "Have I missed something?"

"The other day at the café—"

"Vina," Motts cut her off. "You've already said sorry. I don't require a thousand apologies."

"And we're okay?"

"You're in my cottage—eating more than your

share of my dinner. So, yes." She shifted uncomfortably, not wanting to get into a drawn-out discussion. "We already had that conversation."

"Apologies aren't confrontations, Mottsy."

"Feels like one."

The rest of the evening went smoothly. Vina didn't mention apologising. And Motts eventually settled into their regular routine of dinner and videos.

After Vina left, Motts decided an early night was in order. She made a mug of her dad's hot cocoa, cuddled up with Cactus in bed, and put on a playlist of the Fairyland Cottage on YouTube. She also started a preliminary sketch on a new quilling project—an elaborate harp with autumn leaves for the background.

The following morning, Motts decided to bring her harp design to Looe. Her client was a good friend of her auntie Lily's. She could drop it off at the brewery, then swing by to ask Paisley some questions.

Kill two birds with one stone.

What a terrible phrase.

Why kill birds at all? Birds are brilliant except for the little twit who woke me up this morning by pecking against the window.

Leaving the absurdities of idiomatic expressions

aside, Motts rode her Vespa to Looe. She found her cousin loading up the delivery van. He greeted her with a broad smile.

"Morning." She parked her Vespa on the pavement beside the brewery. "Is Auntie Lily in?"

"Of course; she's in our little lab area. Go on. I've got a meeting with a supplier." River waved her toward the brewery. "Mum's taste-testing a potential new flavour of ale. We're hoping to include it in our next London delivery."

Motts smiled at her cousin's obvious excitement. "We'll be seeing Chen-Mottley in all the London pubs in no time."

"I just hope nothing goes wrong." River closed the rear doors of the van. "We're going to be small fish in a rather large market."

"Makes it easier to swim through traffic jams." Motts shrugged. "Tiny fish can squeeze through all the whales."

"Your mind is always a fun place to be." River grinned at her when she rolled her eyes. "Yes, I'm aware I can't actually be inside your head."

"Good." Motts gave him a quick wave and headed into the building. She made her way through to the lab-like kitchen where her auntie and uncle usually played with flavours and recipes. "I brought you the harp sketch; I wanted your opinion. Where's Uncle Tomato?"

"Chatting with *that* man." Her aunt glared at the right wall as if she could see them through it. "I can't imagine why he's wasting his time."

"What man?" Motts took the glass her aunt shoved across the table at her, exchanging the sample for her sketch. "What's this?"

"Taste first," she ordered while inspecting the sketch. "So talented. I might keep this one for myself when you've finished."

Motts shrugged. She sniffed the beer sample, then sipped slowly. "Oh, lovely. Fruity. Reminds me a little of Ribena. A mildly spicy, beery version."

"Too medicinal?" Her aunt sniffed one of the other cups on the table. "We're experimenting with the levels of spice and blackcurrant."

"Maybe the slightest hint of cough drop?" Motts knew her aunt would appreciate an honest answer. "Only a little, though."

"Hmm. I agree." She nodded firmly, making a notation on the spreadsheet in front of her. "Try this one."

Motts worked her way through six samples before they all began to taste the same. "I should see Uncle Tomato."

"Yes, yes. Off with you. Let me finish up here." She turned her full attention to the spreadsheet once again. "Motts, dear?"

"Yes?"

Her auntie came around the table and kissed her on the forehead. "You're a brilliant, independent young woman. Don't let your mother tell you otherwise."

My mum?

Young woman?

I'm almost forty.

Motts found herself shoved out of the room, and the door closed firmly in her face. "Why is my family so odd?"

There was no answer. Motts sighed. She regretted not going for a second cup of coffee for breakfast.

Having spent loads of time at the brewery, Motts easily found her uncle. He was in an argument with a man she recalled seeing the other day. She tried to remember his name.

The burly man. Heath Miller. What's he doing here?

"Uncle Tom?" Motts stepped into the room as Heath's voice rose to a shout. "Everything okay?"

"Heath wanted advice." Her uncle lifted an arm,

leaving the hug decision up to her. She went over to give him a quick embrace. "What brings you to Looe, young Pineapple?"

"Sketch." Motts stared at the burly man who seemed to loom large in the room despite not being right in front of them. "Shouty advice."

Heath opened his mouth to speak, then seemed to wilt when her uncle cleared his throat loudly. "I'll be going, then. Thanks for the advice."

Motts watched him leave, slamming the door shut behind him. "Sounded more like an argument than advice."

"You never said what brought you here." Her uncle motioned her over to help him lift a box. "Did River ask you over?"

"I brought Auntie Lily a sketch for the harp project. She pressed me into taste-testing service." Motts wiped her now dusty hands off on her cardigan. "Why was Heath Miller really here?"

"Motts."

"Uncle Tomato." She waited stubbornly, hoping he'd give a better answer.

"He wanted my advice on convincing the Bankses to allow him more control at the brewery." Her uncle crossed his arms and stared sternly at her. "Please be careful."

"I'm—"

"You've had a number of close calls." He unfolded his arms and reached out to take her hand in his. "I don't want to be the one phoning your dad up to say we've lost you."

"Sorry," Motts whispered. She didn't mean to make her family worry. "I... sorry?"

"No, don't be. Never mind me, young Pineapple." He pulled her into a gentle hug. "You go be brilliant, brave, and curious."

Wait? What?

Motts was confused.

Mostly. Definitely. Completely confused.

Chuckling to himself, her uncle said his goodbyes and headed out to track down his wife. Motts stared after him. She'd definitely missed something in the conversation as per usual.

Maybe River can explain later.

Time to go.

"You."

Motts twisted around as the door shut behind her. She spied an intimidatingly tall Heath Miller beside her Vespa. "Me?"

"You're the one the Lee bint brought in to find her dead mum." He practically growled at her. "Youths."

"Youths? I'm hardly a youth. I'll be forty soon." Motts eyed him cautiously. She wished he'd move away from her Vespa. "Were you waiting for someone?"

"You should mind your own business." Heath took a step toward her. "You wouldn't want to get hurt."

"The last person to threaten me like that wound up going to prison for murder." Motts didn't think he'd appreciate the blunt honesty. It was definitely time to go. "Do you mind? You're blocking my path."

With Heath momentarily stunned by her casual statement, Motts managed to wheel her Vespa off the pavement. She was already on her way when he came out of his stupor. His shout faded into the noise of the wind rushing by.

The trip home gave her time to consider the suspects in Petunia's death. Her daughter had definitely behaved oddly. Paisley's boyfriend was also high on the list.

Heath had written himself into the mix with his thinly veiled threat. She wondered why he'd thought her uncle could convince the Bankses to promote him. Odd. It was something to ask Paisley about.

There was also Petunia's boyfriend. Motts hadn't

met the man yet. She'd have to watch for him at the funeral.

I'll text River or Vina to see if they'll go with me. They're always better at chatting with strangers.

Motts arrived at the cottage in reasonably good time. The brisk wind had made her long for a cheese toastie with tomato soup. She spotted the tall figure sitting on the bench near the coastal path entrance when she parked her Vespa. "Hello, Teo."

"I brought cookies." Teo lifted a small package. "Vanilin Kiflice—or vanilla crescent cookies. It's a little early in the year for them, but my mother wanted me to have a sweet treat to bring you."

"What brings you to Cornwall? Bit of a drive from Yorkshire." Motts couldn't help feeling a little suspicious. Dempsey had just left for London, and suddenly, Teo had arrived. "Did you have a nice chat with the Londoner?"

"The Londoner?"

"I have a distinct memory of you deriding Detective Inspector Dempsey Byrne as 'the Londoner' when you first met him." Motts walked her Vespa up the path to its usual parking spot. She waited for Teo to join her at the front door of the cottage. "Well?"

"I could've come to visit."

"You have, but something tells me there's more to

it than bringing cookies." Motts fumbled with her keys before finally getting the door open. She laughed when Cactus ignored her to shoot toward Teo like a bullet. "He's missed you."

Cactus had a thing for detectives. He'd made friends with all of them thus far. Motts rolled her eyes and went to heat the kettle up, leaving her cat to enjoy the return of Teo.

"Can you get the fire going?" Motts couldn't stop shivering. She regretted not wearing a heavier coat on her ride. "The wind off the sea turned rather cold. Chilly chilled crispy cold."

And then you can tell me why you've come all the way from Yorkshire without even an email.

I hate surprises.

Even good ones. Throws everything off. Why can't people ever just say what's happening?

Tea. A warm fireplace. Cookies. A purring Cactus.

It would've been the perfect end to Motts's exhausting morning. She'd had enough socialising for the entire week, particularly with the stress of dealing with Heath. While a lovely surprise, Teo was an unwelcome interruption in her plan to spend the rest of the day recovering.

"I won't stay long," Teo promised. He continued

stroking Cactus, who'd stretched out in his arms. "I'm staying in the village for the next few days. Maybe more."

Motts was pleased to see him. She did find the timing of his sudden appearance suspicious. "Yes, but why?"

"I've missed Cornwall—and you." Teo smiled when Cactus grabbed his hand and dragged it over to his head for more attention. "And the cat, of course."

"You haven't made the massive journey from Yorkshire because you missed the sea, me, and a cat." Motts was tired of the way some people in her life seemed to think she didn't see through their flimsy excuses. Her uncle. Teo. Dempsey. Less the latter, she supposed. Dempsey hadn't sugar-coated anything. "You're not usually one to talk around things. Seems to be going around lately."

"Motts."

"What did Dempsey tell you?" She didn't expect a reaction from Teo. He had what her granddad would call a good poker face. "He thinks the killer is after me."

"It's possible."

"Possible plausible politely preys," Motts muttered. She set her tea to one side. "You can't hover around me just in case a serial killer shows up."

"Tired of me already?"

"You have a job. An important one in Yorkshire. And I don't think a babysitter or bodyguard is going to help me." Motts had moved to gain independence. She refused to go backwards. "I'll be careful."

In general, Motts was always cautious. River had accused her of being risk-averse. She never understood why he considered it a negative thing.

What was wrong with not wanting to throw caution to the wind?

Living in Cornwall had taught her several important lessons. One, murderers could find anyone if they tried hard enough. Two, she was strong enough to survive.

She couldn't put her whole life on hold on the off-chance someone might leap out of a hedgerow at her with a knife. *Maybe I can look into some sort of personal safety device. Are those legal? Is there training to turn Cactus into a guard cat?*

"Care to share the joke?" Teo interrupted her laugh.

"Imagining Cactus as an attack cat complete with a set of armour." She grinned at him. "How are you liking Yorkshire?"

"Different. It's a challenge I'm relishing."

Motts had no doubts Teo enjoyed the challenges of heading up his own department. "I'm glad."

"DI Byrne called me." Teo held a hand up to stop her from commenting. "He was concerned about his investigation into the cold case."

"Case seems warmer by the minute." Motts didn't know if they could call a potential serial killer case cold when murders continued to happen. "He called you."

"And asked if I'd swing by Cornwall."

"Swing by? Yorkshire's not exactly around the corner." Motts huffed into her tea. "I won't say I can handle myself against a killer. But you didn't have to drive all the way to Cornwall."

There didn't seem to be much more to say on the subject. Teo didn't have any additional information from Dempsey. Motts decided to talk with the latter herself whenever he returned to Cornwall.

After finishing up tea and massaging Cactus, Teo left to meet up with Perry, likely to discuss the new case at the brewery. Motts promised to relax at home. It had been her plan in the first place.

For the rest of the day, Motts lost herself in her work. She laid out her quilling papers and tools. With her auntie's approval of the sketch, she wanted to get a head start on the autumn motif for the background.

When Vina showed up with supper, Motts had almost finished turning the scrolls of paper into beautifully coloured leaves. She was pleased with the progress.

"Very autumnal." Vina inspected the partially completed art while Motts grabbed two plates from the kitchen. "I found the perfect gift for my nephew."

"You're running with the Cactus being your nephew thing, aren't you?" She set the plates on the table and opened the box from the Ferris Wheel. "What's this?"

"Stone-fired thin crust pizza. Chicken cordon bleu." Vina slid a couple of slices onto her plate. "It sounded interesting."

After a pizza in the garden with Cactus chasing around, they went upstairs to watch videos in the bedroom. Vina stretched out on the bed while Motts sat cross-legged with Cactus in her lap. She pulled out chocolate truffles her granddad had gotten for her a few weeks prior.

"Tell me about Teo."

"What?" Motts frowned in confusion.

"Star-crossed lovers... torn apart by a promotion."

Vina lounged across the end of Motts's bed. She sorted through the box of chocolate truffles. "Are you sure there wasn't a spark when you saw him outside?"

"A spark of annoyance." Motts shrugged. She caught the chocolate Vina tossed at her. "He's lovely."

"But?"

"Lovely like a brilliant friend might be." Motts considered the chocolate in her hand, biting the bottom off to inspect the ganache inside. "Lovely but not in love."

"Ahh, well. Have you seen Beck recently? They made the pizza especially for you."

"They made the pizza because you ordered and paid for it." Motts made a meal out of the truffle, enjoying every last bite. "Why are we friends?"

"Genius recognises genius."

CHAPTER TWELVE

AFTER A DAY SPENT HIDING IN HER COTTAGE AND ignoring anyone who knocked on the door, Motts had recuperated somewhat from the intense energy of the last week. She'd also managed to finish her harp project. Cactus had also enjoyed their time in the garden.

With several days of beautiful weather on the horizon, Motts decided to ride to Looe. She could drop off the harp with her auntie, then go for a walk, maybe see the woods in autumn. Also, if Paisley was at the brewery, Motts might pop over to see her.

Getting up early, Motts rode out to Looe. She dropped the quilled harp off with River since her aunt and uncle weren't in yet. He readily shared his breakfast baos with her.

"The woods? Why on earth would you want to walk this early in the day?" River snagged the last of the steamed buns. "Why bother?"

"I'll send you pictures." Motts hadn't meandered in the Kilminorth Woods since the summer. "It's a beautiful day. I can walk the path in an hour or so. Perfect for this sunny, cool weather."

Leaving her cousin to get to work, Motts stepped outside. She noticed a pale blue car up the street. A shiver went up her spine, and she couldn't help feeling as though the driver was watching her.

Motts lifted her hand to block the glare of sunlight, hoping for a clearer view. She couldn't tell if anyone was even in the car. "Teo's making me paranoid."

The ride to the car park near the entrance to the woods usually relaxed Motts. This time, she found herself periodically glancing over her shoulder. She didn't catch sight of the vehicle, though.

Maybe I should go home. No, I'm being silly. It's fine. The walk in the woods will do me good.

A quarter into the five-kilometre walk, Motts gave up. She turned around to head back to her Vespa. Going further into the woods would likely only stress her further instead of relaxing her as she'd hoped.

Shifting her bag around, Motts fished around to find her phone. She wanted it close at hand in case she had to call for help. *Am I being overly dramatic?*

What's that saying about not being paranoid if people are actually after you?

Motts came out of the woods and stopped dead in her tracks. She eyed a car eerily similar to the one earlier. "It's definitely time to leave."

And maybe I should stop talking to myself as well.

Okay. Stay calm. Get on the Vespa and ride out of the car park straight toward Looe.

If the car followed her, Motts knew reinforcements could be found there. River was at work. Her uncle had likely arrived by now as well.

She'd back her auntie Lily on any day to take someone out. Lily Chen-Mottley was the epitome of the "small but mighty" stereotype. Her family could be formidable when required.

In order to leave the car park, Motts had to ride by the vehicle. She peeked surreptitiously at it on the way by. No one. Teo had definitely made her jumpier than normal.

On the way to the Banks Brewery, Motts went through Looe. She wanted to see if the pale blue car was still parked on the street. It wasn't.

Am I relieved or bewildered?

Can you be both at the same time?

"Motts." Paisley met her in the Coastal Port Brewery car park. She'd obviously seen Motts come up the drive. "Are you ready to continue your investigation? The police aren't offering any answers. In fact, they've been asking me quite rude questions."

And today, we have a posh Paisley.

Mott still didn't know what to make of the ever-changing fashion and mannerisms of Paisley. "Questions about your mum?"

"Personal ones." Paisley didn't elaborate.

Time to change the subject for the moment. Maybe Marnie will know what Perry asked.

"What can you tell me about Heath Miller?" Motts asked. She grabbed her notebook from her bag and flipped to a clean page. "He's the brewmaster, right?"

"Former."

"Oh?" Motts remembered Heath asking her uncle to back him for a promotion at the brewery. "Was it a recent change?"

"Louis's taking over the day-to-day operations at the brewhouse. His parents agreed a younger vision for the future might be best." Paisley puffed up with pride. "I'll be managing the administration side like Mum used to do."

Are you now?

"Congratulations." Motts tried for sincere, though she likely sounded more bewildered. "How are you coping?"

"I'm sorry?"

"The sudden pressure of managing a booming brewery business on the heels of your mother's death. It must be overwhelming." Motts didn't think Paisley found it at all overwhelming. "How did Heath take being sacked?"

"As well as anyone would." Paisley shrugged dismissively. "Why don't you snoop around near the shed? The police have finished up with their investigation."

"Have they?"

"I'm sure you know the way." Paisley spun around and returned to the brewery.

In all her years, Motts hadn't ever met someone quite so mercurial as Paisley. She didn't know what to make of her. Her constant changing also added a layer of confusion to the murder mystery.

How do I decide if she's involved if I can never get a straight answer from her?

What am I even doing here?

Standing in the middle of the employee parking, Motts dithered for several minutes. She could leave. The shed wasn't going to investigate itself.

Her curiosity won out. There wasn't any harm in poking around a little. She hoped.

The sound of a car coming up the lane drew her attention. Motts almost expected to see the pale blue car. She let out a slightly hysterical chuckle when a bright red one appeared instead.

She recognised the man from a photo Paisley had shown her of Petunia's boyfriend—Ernest Herring. "Hello."

"Hello." He paused, getting out of his car, frowning at her. "Have we met?"

"No," Motts admitted. She wondered how to delicately ask him questions. "Were you and Petunia engaged?"

Subtle.

Subtle, Motts.

Subtle suits silly sayings.

"I beg your pardon."

"A friend mentioned you'd gone ring shopping with her." Motts winced when he slammed his door shut. "Must be terrible to lose a fiancée."

"Yes, terrible."

Motts swallowed down her many questions. She didn't believe he'd answer most of them. "When did you see her last?"

"Are you with the police?"

"No."

"Then perhaps you should mind your own business." He strode toward her, stopping to glare down his nose at her. "Despite that, I'll answer your question. Petunia dropped a note through my letterbox, claiming to have gone on a vacation. It happened the night before Paisley came by to ask about her mum. Barely a week or so passed between realising she'd gone missing to her body being found."

Motts opened her mouth to respond, but he walked straight by her into the brewery. "Never mind, then."

Seeing no point in following, Motts walked around the converted farmhouse. She started toward the shed, only for the wall around the pasture to catch her attention. *Oh. I wonder if they found any prints on the binoculars.*

Paisley did say I could explore the property. The wall is on the property. She wasn't specific.

Changing direction, Motts strolled across the

overgrown grass to the wall. She inspected the stacked stones carefully. Nothing stood out to her; the police had likely done a thorough job of searching the area.

After walking along the wall a few times, Motts clambered over it. She walked the meandering path leading away from the property. Even going slowly, she made her way through the heavily wooded area in no time at all, popping out on the narrow lane not far from the entrance to the brewery.

Interesting.

Anyone could've parked down the road and walked through the woods to spy on the brewery. With the binoculars, they'd have been able to see right into Petunia's office. How convenient.

Motts stood on the side of the road for several minutes. "What now?"

No one at the brewery seemed prepared to answer questions. Motts did want to check out Petunia's cottage. She decided to shoot Paisley an email to set up a time to pop by.

First, however, lunch called. The siren cry of fried food made her tummy rumble. She decided to head home; despite his grumpiness, Innis did serve the best fish and chips.

Motts returned home to find an unimpressed Teo once again waiting for her. He was sitting on the wall around her front garden. "I've only got fish for me and the feline."

"Cactus might share." Teo stepped toward her while she wheeled her Vespa up to the usual parking spot. "You should've waited for me."

"Waited? I haven't eaten yet." Motts hefted up the bag. "Rose gave me at least a double portion of chips if you want them."

"Not exactly what I meant." Teo pinched the bridge of his nose. "I could eat chips."

"There's always room for glorious fried potato bliss." Motts fumbled in her pocket for her keys. "Did you want something?"

"You to be more careful."

"I only went to Looe. Kilminorth is lovely at the moment." Motts gestured behind them to the autumnal colours framing her view across the sea and Polperro. "It's magical here this time of year."

Teo sighed so deeply, Motts thought he'd exhaled all of the air in his lungs. "A sight worth seeing."

"Let's have lunch in the garden." Motts enjoyed the salty sea air. She finally turned to get the door open. "Cactus will enjoy the sunlight."

Teo was silent until they were sitting outside in

the comfy lounge chairs. She'd split the extra-large portion of fish and chips between them. "What took you out to Looe?"

"The forest. A harp. A brewery. My cousin." Motts ticked them off on her fingers. She offered Cactus a flake of fish when he leapt into her lap. He looked rather cosy in his cream hoodie—a gift from Vina. "I poked around in the woods a little."

"Where?"

"An unassuming little path off the road out of Looe." Motts picked one of the chips apart, leaving a pile of mush on the plate. "Behind a brewery."

"Motts." Teo shifted around on the chair to sit staring at her. "I didn't think the Chen-Mottley business was near the forest."

"It isn't."

"I wish you'd be more careful."

"I was," Motts insisted. "I even looked both ways when I crossed the street."

"You're taking too many risks." Teo had clearly geared himself up for this argument.

"Riding my Vespa to Looe, visiting my cousin, walking a public path. None of these things are highly dangerous." Motts refused to change her entire life. "I am being careful."

Careful-ish.

Deciding not to mention the potentially suspicious vehicle to Teo, Motts figured Dempsey might handle the news better. She assumed, at least. Arguing over it felt pointless to her.

Why bother? It never seemed to change anyone's mind. She didn't understand what they wanted. Was she supposed to stay in the cottage and never leave?

It reminded her too much of living in London with her parents.

After an hour or so, Teo left to meet up with Inspectors Ash and Yuen. Motts didn't know what to make of the awkward lunch together. What had he expected?

Deciding brooding wouldn't help at all, Motts carried Cactus into the cottage. The past week had been an odd roller coaster. She struggled to process any of it.

Not the update in Jenny's case.

Or Paisley.

Or Petunia's bizarre manner of death.

And Teo's return had definitely not helped.

"Time for tea, toast, and a hot water bottle." Motts set Cactus down on his bed by the window with his turtle plushie, a poor substitute for his best friend, Moss. "Mysteries muddle my...."

Meow.

"Yes, yes, I ran out of ideas. Don't be a critic." Motts filled the kettle up and flipped the switch. "Mysteries muddle memories most mindfully."

Still needs work.

CHAPTER THIRTEEN

"Morning."

"Hello." Motts came down the last of the steps leading from her cottage to the village. She fell into step with Beck, who was on their way past. "You're up early."

"Grabbing a coffee before I head to the restaurant. We're testing out a few new recipes this morning to decide if we want them on the menu." Beck walked on the cobblestone street, leaving Motts to have the narrow pavement. "Have you had brekkie yet?"

"No."

"Care to join me?" Beck asked. "I planned to stop by Griffin Brews."

"Sure." Motts had been on her way there

anyway. "I usually pop by for coffee or tea."

If I'm not hiding in the cottage eating more lemon curd on toast than is healthy for a person. Don't be weird. Don't make the conversation weird. You can handle small talk.

Who am I kidding?

I can't handle small talk.

"Well, he's tall."

Motts glanced down the sidewalk to find Teo waiting outside the café. "Teo Herceg. Detective Inspector."

"Explains the spiky vibe." Beck grinned at her. "What do you recommend for breakfast?"

"It's all brilliant. I'm fond of their pasties." Motts waved at Teo, who offered a smile before turning a curious glance toward Beck. "Morning. Have you met Beck? They run the new bistro down the street. We're having breakfast."

See? All those hours of practising introducing random people to one another in the mirror paid off. I even got names right.

For some reason Motts didn't understand, Teo reacted in surprise to the last part of her introduction. He began asking Beck loads of questions. *Is he interrogating them?*

What the....

"Oh, look, Vina has a new breakfast treat to try." Motts caught Beck's sleeve to drag them over to the counter. Teo followed at a slower pace. "What's this?"

"Well, hello, you two. Or, three?" Vina nodded to them with a wide grin. "Having fun, Mottsy?"

Closing her eyes for a moment, Motts counted to ten. She opened them, ordered her usual tea, and tried one of the new roasted curry potato pasties. To her surprise, both Teo and Beck followed her over to a table after they'd ordered their own breakfast.

Is this weird?

This is definitely weird.

The pasty went down far more quickly than anticipated. Motts excused herself from the bizarre conversation happening around her. Vina was still snickering at the counter.

"Thanks for the morning entertainment." Vina slid another pasty onto her plate. "Teo certainly seems to be fascinated with Beck."

"It is odd, right?" Motts didn't know what to make of the morning thus far. "I've missed something."

"I think Teo's jealous of your date."

"Wait? What date? We're having breakfast, is

all." Motts hadn't considered it a dating thing. "Why would he be jealous?"

"You'll have to ask him. And yes, I'm fairly certain Beck thought they'd asked you on an impromptu date." Vina leaned across the counter to whisper. "I heard some gossip. Louis Banks is home from university."

"Interesting." Motts picked up the pasty to have a bite.

"And, rumour also claims he was in Looe a week ago or so." Vina grabbed her phone and showed Motts a few photos on an Instagram page. "Sure looks like him enjoying Talland Bay."

"Is it a rumour when you found the photo?" Motts peeked over her shoulder to find Beck and Teo still in conversation. "How do I make them stop being weird?"

"You being friends with all of your exes is weird," Vina teased.

"You're one of my exes."

"I don't count." Vina waved a hand airily. "Or maybe I'm the only one who does."

"Do you practise making no sense?" Motts grabbed the plate and smiled when Nish wandered by to drop a freshly baked chocolate hazelnut scone on it. "Want to visit Paisley with me later?"

"How about for lunch? We can try the new Thai place."

After nodding her agreement, Motts returned to the table with the rest of her breakfast. She took a seat, pointedly ignoring the stilted conversation between Teo and Beck. They could sort things out for themselves.

"Sorry. We got distracted," Beck apologised after a few minutes. "His parents know one of my mentors from my time in Paris."

"Small world." Motts focused on her scone, trying to identify the hint of flavour underneath the darker chocolate and hazelnut. "Raspberry. Raspberry and caramel."

"What?"

"This scone. It's divine." Motts twisted around to give a watching Nish two thumbs up. "I'm going to want a dozen."

Nish lifted up a box. "Already ahead of you."

"My friends are the best friends," Motts said firmly.

After a few moments of silence from Teo, he excused himself. Motts stared after him. He'd been decidedly odd since returning to Cornwall.

"He cares about you." Beck drew her attention.

"I've rarely been grilled so subtly yet terrifyingly in my life. Not on a first date."

"This was a date?" Motts could hear Vina snickering. She made a mental note to murder her best friend. "Not simply breakfast?"

"I'm fine with whatever makes you more comfortable."

"Breakfast with a hint of something more in the future." Motts wasn't opposed to an actual date with Beck. She didn't know if her current emotional state could handle it, though. "We'll talk."

"Later, though. I've got a restaurant to run." Beck winked at her, gathered up their coffee, and headed out of the café.

Motts slouched so far down in the chair that she almost slid off. "What is even happening?"

"Dating troubles?" Nish came over to clean up the table. "Want some advice?"

"No."

"Brilliant. Beck's worth a date, I think."

"Wonderful. Go away now." Motts did her breathing exercises, trying to clear her thoughts.

Moving from the front of the café into the table in the corner of the kitchen, Motts made a few lists to help centre her thoughts. Leena and Nish periodically popping over to give her tasting samples of their bakes and treats didn't hurt either. She revelled in the simple warmth of their welcome.

Her attention turned to the murder mystery. If Louis Banks was in Cornwall when Petunia went missing, why had he lied about it? Why claim he'd been at university?

Was he involved in the murder?

Was Paisley?

Control of the brewery could definitely be claimed as a motive. Everyone agreed Petunia tended to be unmoveable in her opinions. She had an iron grip on running the place.

Paisley and Louis had a vision for the future but no control. Heath Miller stood in their way. He'd been fired.

Had Petunia been murdered for the same reason?

Sacrificed to their ambition?

Finishing up her thoughts on paper, Motts returned home with her box of scones and a treat for Cactus. She spent the rest of the morning checking her email, sketching out paper bouquet ideas, and watching Cactus traipse in the garden. Vina arrived at noon on the dot, honking her horn for Motts to join her.

"I am a terrible liar."

Motts stared at Vina. "Hello, terrible liar."

"Did you steal my dad's joke book?" Vina waited for her to get situated in the passenger seat. "Teo popped by the café to see if you were still there."

"Okay."

"And I panicked."

"Why?" Motts repeatedly yanked on her seat belt. "Why does your car hate me?"

"Honestly. You and Nish. Neither of you can work a seat belt." Vina reached over to give her a hand. "There. Now, back to lies and panic."

"And apparently, Teo. Shouldn't we be driving?"

"Yes, about that." Vina glanced behind them before reversing slowly down the lane. "Teo might meet us in Looe."

"There goes our chance to chat with Louis and Paisley." Motts didn't think anyone would volunteer answers with Teo looming over them. "I wonder what Detective Inspector Yuen thinks of his temporary return, since she basically has his position."

"I've no idea. I doubt she minds. He's only here for a few days."

"Would you?"

"Mind? I don't know." Vina got the vehicle turned around and headed out of Polperro. "You realise Teo still has feelings for you."

"Well, we are friends."

Vina turned to stare at her for a second. "I can never tell if you're being purposefully obtuse or not."

"We broke up. Cordially. We're friends. He's not harbouring some...." Motts didn't even know how to end the sentence. "Who do you think killed Petunia?"

"Subtle change of subject." Vina held up a hand when Motts went to respond. "My money's on Paisley, possibly with the help of Louis. How about you?"

Motts watched Vina manoeuvre her car around a lorry on the narrow lane. "Could you try not to kill us with your driving?"

"She who doesn't drive a car shouldn't throw stones."

"Not how the phrase goes." Motts tried not to cling to the armrest. "I'm holding out my opinion until I've officially met Petunia's boyfriend. He might prove to be guilty. All those crime podcasts we've listened to. How many times does it wind up being the person's partner who did them in?"

"Too many. It's almost enough to make you reconsider a relationship." Vina slammed on the brakes, narrowly avoiding a stopped car. "Oi."

Motts closed her eyes and tried to remember how

to breathe. She'd forgotten how stressful driving with Vina could be. "You can't blame them for your driving."

"You're worse than driving with my parents. Killjoy." Vina honked the horn repeatedly. "Are you praying under your breath?"

"Some people swear by it." Motts was beginning to regret all of her life choices. "Can you get us to Looe without wrecking in a spectacular fashion?"

The rest of the drive went smoothly. Motts was able to relax when Vina calmed down and quit pretending they were on the autobahn. They pulled into the Coastal Port Brewery employee parking in a relatively short time.

Shorter than if Motts had ridden her Vespa or been the passenger in any other car.

"I thought you told Teo." Motts didn't see his vehicle anywhere. "Did you tell him when we'd planned to meet up?"

"I may have said we planned to be at the restaurant around one. Ow." Vina rubbed her arm where Motts had smacked her. "What? You distracted me, and I couldn't finish telling you how my conversation with him went."

"Vina."

Arguing with Vina never turned out well. Motts

decided not to bother. She got out of the car and hunted in her bag for her notebook.

They went straight into the brewery. Paisley met them before they made it too far inside. She led them up the stairs and into what had been her mother's office.

Stepping into the room, Motts did a double take. The office had gone through quite a makeover. If she hadn't seen the original, she'd never have known it hadn't been like it currently was.

The sparse and functional room had been transformed into a stylish, modern office with a pastel hint. Paisley had certainly made herself at home. There wasn't a sign of Petunia anywhere aside from the desk and chair that hadn't been swapped out.

"You've been busy." Motts glanced up to find Paisley hadn't been alone in her office. "Hello. Have we met?"

"I don't think we've had the pleasure. Louis Banks." He strode forward, wrapping an arm around Paisley's shoulders. "How can we help you both?"

"I had a few questions, if you don't mind." Motts flipped to the page in her notebook where she'd jotted them down. "For both of you, actually. Also, would it be possible to check out your mum's cottage at some point?"

"I suppose." Paisley sighed exaggeratedly.

Posh Paisley has made an appearance once again.

Motts decided to ignore the mannerism changes. "Brilliant. It might help me discover more about who did this."

"How about this afternoon? We've got a meeting at noon, but later this afternoon should be fine." Louis interjected into the conversation. "Right, Paisley?"

"Of course." She nodded.

Why is everything about this murder and the people involved so decidedly odd?

Seeing no point in trying to decipher the complexities of someone else's relationship, Motts opted to keep the conversation on track. She wanted to know more about Louis. When had he last visited Paisley?

"Can you tell me when you were last in Polperro?" Motts didn't want to ask him about the photo outright. He'd likely either refuse to answer or lie. "It must be hard being so far away from Paisley, your family, and the brewery."

"It is, though one hopes the education I'm getting will help the business." Louis leaned down to give Paisley a kiss. "We see each other as much as possible. To answer the question, I haven't been to Cornwall since my last break from university. Several months at least. It's a bit of a drive."

"We're friends on Insta." Vina spoke before Motts could react. "Saw you posting last week about Talland Bay. It's beautiful this time of year."

"Old photo from the summer." Louis smiled down at Paisley. "We were celebrating an anniversary."

Right.

The summer.

Vina's probably not the only liar today.

All of Motts's other questions received similarly evasive answers. For someone who'd asked her to look into her mother's death, Paisley didn't seem too bothered to cooperate. Motts wondered if she'd been more open with the police.

I really need to pop by the bridal shop. Marnie always has the best gossip to share.

CHAPTER FOURTEEN

"What now?" Vina leaned against her vehicle, tossing her keys casually into the air. "We could snoop around the brewery."

"Maybe later." Motts checked the time on her phone. She'd given up wearing watches; they made her skin itch. "Aren't we supposed to be meeting up with Teo for lunch?"

The drive into the village to find a parking spot went more sedately than their mad dash from Polperro to the brewery. Motts was grateful. She didn't think her stomach would appreciate eating after a chaotic adventure involving Vina's vehicle skills.

While they waited for Teo, Motts thought over the conversation with Paisley and Louis. She didn't want to believe they were killers. But they had a motive.

And they'd definitely lied.

"Does Nish still have the friend who claimed to be able to tell what month it was based on the position of the sun?" Motts remembered him mentioning her. She studied weather or something at university and occasionally worked with the police. "Maybe she could tell us if Louis's photo came from the summer."

"I can't remember her name. I'll text Nish." Vina peered around, then waved with the hand not holding her phone. "Inspector Tall, Dark, and Broody has arrived."

Motts covered her face with her hands. "Can you not? He might hear you."

"And?" Vina checked her nails carefully. She kept them trimmed close for baking. "He's not even remotely bothered about what I think."

"Can you, for one lunch, not be exhausting?" Motts pleaded. "I'm officially at capacity for trying to decipher when someone's joking."

She straightened immediately, all hint of joking swept away. "We can always get lunch to go. It's going to be crowded. Why don't we have a take-away? Teo can follow us either home or to the beach.

What about Hannafore? It's rarely busy this time of year."

"I don't want to be difficult."

"You're not being difficult. The world is loud, chaotic, and rarely accommodating. You more than deserve the right to want to lower the volume." Vina summoned one of the employees wandering by. She had a hushed conversation while Motts retreated to the muffled calm of her headphones. "Want me to order for you?

Motts nodded. She trusted Vina to know what she'd enjoy eating. "Fine."

"Not late, am I?" Teo had finally made his way across the crowded restaurant. His eyes narrowed, obviously sensing tension at the table. "What's happened?"

Motts pulled the headphones off to hear him better. "A lot of noise."

Without the noise cancellation, Motts heard a cascading crescendo of sound. The cosy restaurant turned into a claustrophobic cave. She listened to every single conversation happening around her amplified in stereo.

A car alarm sounded outside. Pans crashed in the kitchen. A glass dropped somewhere in the distance.

Holding onto her headphones loosely, Motts

tried to breathe through the tidal wave of feeling overwhelmed. A light flickered overhead through the spinning blades of a fan. She closed her eyes, but it didn't help.

"Pick one of the salads for me." Teo gave Vina his order. He guided Motts out of the restaurant. "Why don't we get you in my car?"

With her headphones back on, Motts sank into the sudden escape from the sound. It no longer felt like someone was stabbing her in the ears. She owed Dempsey a massive thank you for the gift of noise cancellation.

It helped immensely.

Teo got into the driver seat after a while. "Vina's getting lunch. She'll meet us at the Hannafore Beach car park."

The drive took no time at all. Teo found a spot quickly in the empty car park and got out to give her space to herself. She appreciated his thoughtfulness.

Motts rested her head against the window, staring out at the sea. The tide was out, so water flowed around the rocks, leaving pools in some places. "I need to take better care of myself."

And learn to say no.

And learn it's okay for me to not be able to cope.

And maybe stop talking to myself.

The rock formations dotting the beach reminded her of knights guarding the Cornish coastline. Motts had tried climbing them as a child, winding up with scraped arms and legs for her trouble. Her mum had been horrified.

The rumbling of her tummy drew her out of her thoughts and the vehicle. Motts kept her headphones on and went to join Vina and Teo. The former held a box out to her.

"You've got their deep-fried pork on toast and a satay salad." Vina went back to her own lunch.

It was nice. Lunch by the sea in companionable quiet. She appreciated the silence, particularly as Vina tended to find it challenging to sit in her own thoughts.

"Thank you." Motts adjusted the noise cancellation to low and carefully packed up her empty lunch packet.

With Vina needing to get back to work, she left Teo and Motts at the beach. They continued to sit in silence for several minutes. He was clearly letting her decide what came next.

Motts eased her hands into the sleeves of her oversized jumper. She wrapped her arms around herself. "Why were you so strange at breakfast?"

Teo breathed out deeply, staring out at the

ocean. "You always surprise me with your directness."

"Life's always easier when you get straight to the point." Motts had learned the hard way that often, being direct led to hurt feelings and confusion. "Most of the time."

"I wanted to make sure Beck wasn't taking advantage."

"Taking advantage of what?" Motts glanced over at him. "Breakfast? Don't be inscrutable."

"Inscrutable?" Teo gave her a wry smile. "Let me sort out my own feelings. They're not your responsibility. And I'm sorry if I made your morning uncomfortable."

"Weird, not uncomfortable." Motts wanted to understand what had happened. It always bothered her when she knew she'd missed something. "But why act so strange?"

"Despite appearances, even I can behave irrationally. I haven't seen you in a while, and the first time I see you when I visit, you're on a date," Teo stated simply.

"First, I didn't know it was a date," Motts pointed out. "And second, you saw me the day before."

"You'd have been a brilliant detective with your need to be precise."

"I'd have been a terrible police officer." Motts could admit, at least to herself, she enjoyed investigating crimes even when they terrified her. She also knew the justice system wasn't always just, which angered her greatly. "Have you heard anything about the recent murder?"

"Motts."

"Would you rather continue our unnecessary and awkward conversation about dating?" Motts certainly wanted to change the subject even if he didn't. "Well?"

"Hughie and Perry filled me in over a beer last night. They introduced me to the new detective as well, Rebecca Yuen. She'll do well here." Teo stood up, stretching out his legs. "Why don't we walk on the beach before I give you a lift home?"

Emotions were odd things. Motts decided one mystery was more than enough. She could focus on Petunia.

"How do you filter through suspects when everyone seems guilty?" Motts hopped over a rock formation. "And I do mean everyone."

"Shouldn't the goal be to avoid dead bodies?"

"I try to avoid the dead. They keep popping up. Sometimes, they're not even in the ground," Motts complained. "Could you ignore a mystery that landed in your lap?"

"I'm a detective inspector. I'm not supposed to." Teo bent down to pick up a stone and inspected it. "Trusting your instincts helps, though evidence has to back up those feelings. Take each person individually and go down the path until you either eliminate them from the list or prove they're involved."

"Is that what you do?"

"I'm not giving you a crash course on investigating a crime." Teo shut down the conversation with a firm shake of his head. "Let's get you back to your cottage. Those rain clouds are getting closer."

Thankfully for Motts, the drive to Polperro went slower with Teo behind the wheel. He didn't try any sharp manoeuvres on the road. She was still happy to get to her cottage.

Motts waved her goodbyes after she got out of the car. She didn't have the energy for further chatting. Cactus sat by the door, waiting for her when she opened it. "You'll have to do without your Teo. He's heading home tomorrow morning."

Meow.

"You'll survive." Motts grabbed her laptop and a snack for Cactus and headed upstairs to crawl into bed. "Time for a true crime podcast. I need ideas."

Meow.

"You're right. There is a new episode of Osian and Danny's London Crime Podcast." Motts settled into bed with Cactus curled up on her pillow.

"This is Oz and D. Welcome to another episode of our London Crime Podcast."

Motts adjusted the volume on her headphones. "Wonder if I could email them about Jenny's case? It happened in London. They might draw more attention to it, maybe trigger someone's memory."

Halfway through the podcast, Motts remembered she'd intended to pop by the bridal shop to see Marnie. She grabbed her phone to send a message to see if they could chat the following morning. A few minutes later, she received a response.

Marnie: Yes, and I've got an intriguing bit of news for you.

Motts: Oh?

Marnie: You'll see tomorrow.

Motts: Marnie.

Marnie: Must run. It's date night in the Ash cottage.

CHAPTER FIFTEEN

"WHAT—" MOTTS CRASHED OUT OF BED, bashing her elbow against the nightstand on the way down. She sat up slowly and attempted to clear the fog of sleep out of her mind. "Cactus?"

A loud thud hit her window, causing her to jolt for a second time. Motts fumbled around before finding her phone and sending a panicked text to Hughie. She opened the security app, switching on the bright spotlight in the garden.

Motts crept forward to peer out the window. She noticed a smear of something streaked down the glass. It had a yellowish tinge. "Why in the world is someone throwing produce at my window?"

Meow.

"Don't worry. I'm going to wait for Hughie."

Motts gripped her phone tightly while tiptoeing downstairs with Cactus at her heels. "There's no one on the CCTV footage. Maybe the light scared them off."

Even with every light in the cottage on, Motts still huddled by the front door. She watched the live feeds from the cameras. In no time at all, she spotted Hughie's vehicle coming up the lane.

Motts hesitantly opened the door and breathed a sigh of relief. "Sorry to drag you out of bed. It's half-past the dead of night."

"It's what I'm here for." Hughie brushed off her apology with a concerned smile. "What's going on then?"

Leading him through the cottage, Motts explained her rude awakening. Hughie immediately went out to see for himself. She followed him from a distance.

Cactus remained inside. He'd hopped up to observe them from his favourite cushion by the living room window. Motts thought he was the cleverest of them.

"You should've stayed inside." Hughie flashed his torch in her direction. "I'm not seeing anyone. Smells sweet—like overly ripe fruit."

"Why is...." Motts took a moment to compose her

thoughts. "Are you saying someone chucked rotten fruit at my cottage? Teens having a laugh, maybe?"

"Probably." Hughie walked along the fence line, using his torch to check more closely. "They must've disappeared down the coastal path."

"Pineapple."

"Pardon?"

"Pineapple." Motts held up a dripping, smelly chunk. "Want it as evidence?"

"I'll pass. Not sure even the best of techs could get a fingerprint from a pineapple. You might be able to compost it." Hughie continued peering over the top of the fence. "You hitting the lights likely scared them off."

"Maybe the camera caught something? I haven't checked yet. Risky running along the path at night." Motts wrapped her robe more tightly around herself; the biting wind coming up off the sea went right through her. "Come inside. I'll make us hot chocolate while you watch the CCTV footage."

With Hughie sitting at the table watching the CCTV feed on her laptop, Motts focused her nervous energy elsewhere. She chopped up some of the milk and dark chocolate Teo had brought her, mixing it with double cream and milk in a pan on the hob. Her dad always believed in making hot chocolate a special treat.

Five minutes of her hot chocolate ritual did wonders for her anxiety. Motts carried a mug over to Hughie, who accepted with a grateful smile. He replayed part of the footage for her, showing a shadowy figure flinging pineapple at the cottage.

"Can you send me this video? I don't recognise the person, but I'd like to show this to Inspector Ash." Hughie took a tentative sip of the hot chocolate. "You make the best hot choccy."

"Thanks." Motts preened at the praise. "Sure you don't want to show the video to Inspector Yuen? Are you blushing? River's right. You do like her."

"And?"

"It's sweet. You deserve someone lovely in your life." Motts greatly appreciated the kind giant of a constable who went out of his way to help his neighbours. "Have you asked her out?"

"She's only just come home."

Motts didn't know what that had to do with asking her out. "I imagine her being here would make the process easier, not harder."

Then again, what did Motts know? Her dating history, such as it was, hadn't often involved asking someone out and certainly not a lifelong crush. She imagined Hughie felt pressure to get things right.

Why did romance tend to make people behave so oddly?

They watched the security footage multiple times while sipping hot chocolate. Neither of them recognised the person. The video simply wasn't clear enough.

Finishing his hot chocolate, Hughie made his way home. Motts triple-checked all the locks and windows. She left several lights on and hunkered in upstairs, watching the live camera feeds until she fell into an uneasy sleep.

Her doorbell woke her up several hours later. Motts trudged downstairs, almost tripping over Cactus, who complained loudly. She managed to get safely to the door without injuring either of them.

"Well, you certainly had a rough night. Hughie suggested you might appreciate a pick-me-up this morning." Marnie lifted up a basket. "I've brought raspberry muffins, lemon curd, and a thermos of your favourite latte from Griffin Brews. Nish made it especially."

"Many words," Motts mumbled. She stumbled away from the door, assuming Marnie would follow. "Too many words."

"Here, love. The latte will help." Marnie held out the thermos. "Drink up. I'll tell you about all the latest village gossip."

After a mug and a half of tea, Motts was more awake and less annoyed at being so. She grabbed a second muffin and slathered it with a healthy dose of lemon curd. Marnie continued to nibble on her own breakfast treat.

"So?" Motts prompted when Marnie seemed content to eat breakfast in silence. "Gossipy stuff?"

"Our teddy bear constable was seen having dinner with a certain newly arrived detective inspector last night."

"Seen by whom?"

"Well, me and Perry. We invited them both to dinner in the hopes they'd realise what everyone else sees." Marnie laughed when Motts rolled her eyes. "I thought I'd ease you into the gossip."

"Really?"

"Rumour also has it your detective inspector headed home this morning." Marnie observed her carefully, likely hoping for a reaction. "Everything okay?"

"He's not my anything. Well, he's a friend." Motts casually bit into the muffin, enjoying the tart bite of the lemon curd. "Why is everyone so obsessed with this? People date. They stop dating. They remain friends. It's not earth-shattering news."

"Fair enough." Marnie eased the thermos closer. "Top up on the tea?"

"Was that all the gossip?"

"Hardly. Heard something about Ernest Herring." Marnie laughed when Motts sat up straight in her chair, almost dislodging a sleeping Cactus. "I thought you'd be interested. He was spotted having a spectacular row with Paisley outside her mum's cottage. Things were thrown. Police were called. All quite dramatic."

"At Petunia's cottage?" Motts considered this while munching on her muffin. "Odd. Do you know what the row was about?"

"Something about removing property. No idea who was removing what, though." Marnie shrugged. "Perry hadn't heard anything this morning."

"I'm supposed to go see Petunia's place. Vina messaged me to say she'd called Paisley to put it off until today." Motts eyed the last of the muffins. How many were too many? "Maybe I can find out what the row was about."

Finishing up breakfast, Marnie said her good-byes. Motts set Cactus up with his own meal. She went out into the garden to check on her plants and see if anything showed up in the daylight.

All her plants seemed to be doing fine. Motts found several remnants from the early morning attack. She gathered up the pineapple, dumping it into her compost.

It didn't feel like a random attack. Throwing pineapple at Pineapple had definitely been a choice. Motts went through the garden gate to peruse the coastal path.

Her search was fruitless. Motts didn't see anything out of the ordinary after inspecting every section of her fence. She found nothing.

Motts walked back to the gate, pausing when she spotted something in the wall on the other side of the path. A flash of something wedged between two of the stones. She grabbed her phone out of her pocket and snapped a few photos of it.

Gloves.

I need gloves.

Racing back into the cottage, Motts dug around in her backpack for a pair of disposable gloves. She'd gotten them from Nish, who occasionally used them to keep his fingers clean at the bakery. Cactus watched her but didn't budge off his bed when she retraced her steps outside.

After a few breaths to calm her nerves, Motts strode straight over to the wall. She crouched down and gently tugged at the item. With a bit of effort, she eased out a frayed friendship bracelet.

Motts sat down hard on the path, grasping desperately at the bracelet. "No."

The colours took her breath away. Yellows, greens, and browns in a chevron pattern. Motts fingered a loose embroidery thread. She'd bet her cottage the bracelet was Jenny's.

She remembered making it.

One hellish summer when her mum had decided Motts wasn't learning how to socialise, she'd been forced to attend a day camp for several months. It had been a nightmare.

The friendship bracelets had kept her going, though. Motts had made one for herself, Jenny, her dad, cousin, most of her family, really. They'd all been made in the colours of a pineapple because it made her laugh.

The only thing to make her laugh that summer.

She hadn't thought of the bracelets in years. Jenny had worn it everywhere when they'd returned to school. Had the killer taken it off her after murdering her as a memento?

Returning to the cottage, Motts placed the

bracelet in a little container for Dempsey. He'd be interested. She made sure to lock the back door securely.

They were right.

Whoever killed Jenny had definitely set their sights on her.

CHAPTER SIXTEEN

"Have you seen a ghost?" Nish greeted Motts when she walked into the café. "Motts?"

"Mottsy?" Vina came around the counter, rushing over to loop her arm around Motts and guide her through the Employees Only door into the kitchen. "Sit, sit. What's wrong?"

Shaking her head, Motts dropped into one of the chairs. She readily accepted the mug of tea from Nish. The twins hovered for a moment before Caden chased his children out front and back to work.

He returned to sit across from her. "Want to talk about it?"

"Not really."

"Well, enjoy the warmth of our hearth." Caden

reached over to pat her hand gently. "Drink your tea. I'll keep the troublesome twins busy for a few minutes."

Tea solved a multitude of problems. It didn't stop a serial killer, however. Motts set the mug down and fished her phone out, sending Dempsey a message with an image of what she'd found and where.

His response came in quickly. He was on his way to Cornwall, which explained Teo's sudden departure. Did the two detective inspectors think the local police couldn't keep her safe?

"Well?" Vina snuck into the kitchen. "Nish's keeping Dad busy with a non-existent issue with the accounting software."

"Did you hear about—"

"Someone throwing pineapple at your cottage? Hughie was here this morning. Heard all about it," Vina interrupted her.

"I found a bracelet on the wall along the coastal path." Motts showed her the photo she'd sent Dempsey. "I think whoever threw the pineapple left it for me to find."

"A friendship bracelet?" Vina grabbed her phone to get a closer look. "I haven't seen one of these since the sixth form. We used to make them for our besties."

"Yes." Motts wrapped her fingers tightly around the mug, trying to draw in some of the warmth. "This one is a little more special because I made it."

"Pardon?"

"I made it." Motts sloshed her tea when Vina grabbed her arm. "Oi."

"Sorry." Vina grabbed a tea towel from a nearby counter and mopped up the tea. "You made it?"

"For Jenny. At a summer camp aeons ago." She stared into what was left of her tea. "I think the killer was taunting me. Teasing me like Cactus would one of his catnip toys."

"You're going to be fine." Vina's hands trembled while she twisted the towel. "Maybe you should stay—"

"No," Motts interrupted firmly. "My cottage has a fancy security system. Cameras, alarms, lights. I've even got my own attack cat."

"Cactus is *not* going to protect you from a killer." Vina swept her hair off her shoulders, tying it up in an effortless bun. "Why don't I stay in your spare room for a few days?"

"Because you'd provide what?" Motts didn't think Vina would be the first choice for a bodyguard. "Are you going to be a layer of defence?"

"Mottsy."

"Motts?" Nish poked his head into the kitchen. "River's here. Said he's promised to give you a lift to Looe."

Giving Vina a hopefully reassuring hug, Motts followed Nish out of the kitchen. She thanked him for providing a needed interruption. He greeted River with a kiss, then left the cousins alone.

"Rough morning?"

Motts collapsed into the passenger seat with a groan. "You heard about the pineapple."

"Of course. Pretty sure everyone who knows you aside from your parents has heard about it. Mum's decided to cook up a feast for you because food cures all problems. Obvs." River chuckled. He leaned over when she held out her phone. "Friendship bracelet? I haven't seen one of those in ages. Wait. Didn't you make me one of these in the exact same colours?"

"I made this one as well." Motts put her phone away. "Found it behind the cottage. It was Jenny's. I'm sure of it."

"Jenny's?"

They drove to Looe in silence. River was clearly processing the implications of the bracelet. Motts couldn't blame him; she still hadn't. A few simple embroidery threads had never seemed so threatening.

"Maybe we don't mention the bracelet to my parents." River made an excellent point. Her aunt and uncle might be less prone to overreaction than hers, but still. "Dad would call yours, who'd tell your mum."

"And she'd try to drag me home." Motts could imagine precisely how her mum might react. "As if I'd be safer there, a stone's throw from where Jenny was murdered."

"I see Paisley and Louis." River pointed across the street from where he'd parked. "Ready to play Sherlock Holmes?"

Motts hesitated before unbuckling her seat belt. "What do you think about Louis?"

"Privileged prat who thinks the world owes him respect." River shrugged. "I can't say I know him well despite our parents being in the same business community. He was always away at boarding school or drinking with his equally posh mates."

"Do you think Paisley puts on a mask to be around him and his circle?" Motts thought it would explain the changes in appearance and mannerisms. "She might believe he'd break up with her."

"Possibly."

"I want to believe in the shy, sweet woman who rushed to my cottage worried about her missing mum." Motts watched as the couple engaged in an intense conversation. Louis was leaning in close, gesturing wildly, while Paisley had her arms wrapped tightly around herself. "Okay. Let's see what they're up to."

The conversation screeched to a halt when Motts and River crossed the road. The couple were all smiles. Motts thought the expressions looked painted on by a terrible artist, stretching their grins too far.

What in the world were they talking about when we walked up? I suppose I could ask.

Odds of them telling me the truth? Nil. Odds of my asking without a healthy dose of unnecessary awkwardness? Also nil.

"Morning," Louis greeted jovially. He shook River's hand while nodding to Motts when she shoved her hands in her pocket. "We've left the place as is. We wouldn't want to ruin your little attempts to investigate."

Little attempts to investigate?

Smug prat.

River continued to shake Louis's hand far longer than Motts thought necessary. "Good to see you, old chap."

Motts stared at her cousin in disbelief. There

was definitely some animosity between the two. She made a mental note to ask him about it later. "Right. Okay. How about we check out the cottage? No point in standing outside all morning."

Paisley twisted around and led them up the walk. "Mum kept her cottage rather immaculate. I'm not sure you'll find much."

"The police have combed over the place quite thoroughly." Louis had a definite edge to his words. "It's a lovely cottage—practically market ready."

"Market ready?" Motts kept her attention on Paisley, noting her increasing uneasiness. "Are you selling your mum's cottage?"

"I don't...." Paisley stumbled when Louis wrapped an arm around her shoulders and tugged her closer to him. "We're considering our options."

Our?

Exchanging a glance with River, Motts followed the couple up the steps of Petunia's house. It took a moment to get inside since Louis seemed unwilling to let go of Paisley. His behaviour was decidedly odd.

The cottage was pristine. Immaculate. It belonged on the cover of a magazine. Motts doubted they'd find a speck of dust even with a white glove.

Motts did a circuit around the living room, then

continued down the hall to Petunia's bedroom. "River?"

"What?" He came up behind her, resting a hand on her shoulder. "Holy—"

As clinically clean as the cottage had been, Petunia's bedroom was a tip. Clothes were strewn everywhere. A chest of drawers and a bedside table had been knocked over, with all the contents dumped on the floor.

"I'm texting Hughie. He can let the detectives know about this if they don't already." River shook his head at the mess. "Computer's gone."

"How do you know?"

He pointed to several wires on the desk in the corner of the room. "I'm guessing a laptop unless she'd taken it to the brewery. Or maybe she had one for personal use?"

"Oh my god." Paisley swayed behind Motts, gripping the doorframe to stay on her feet. "What happened?"

Motts peered over her shoulder at her, wondering how honest the reaction was. "You didn't notice the mess when you were here yesterday?"

"I wasn't...."

"Weren't you here with Ernest Herring?" Motts

asked when Paisley trailed off. "Chatting about your mum's funeral, maybe?"

"I couldn't bring myself to go beyond the living room." Paisley's voice trembled with each word. "Ernie was already here when I arrived. He had a box. A box! We haven't.... I haven't decided what to do with any of Mum's stuff. He refused to show me what he'd taken."

"So, you had a row?" Motts awkwardly patted her on the shoulder. "I'm so sorry about your mum."

Paisley threw her arms around Motts, beginning to sob uncontrollably. "She's really gone."

Standing with her arms stiffly at her sides, Motts didn't know what to do. She tried not to move. Paisley eventually cried herself out and stepped back.

"I'm not usually so emotionally overwrought." Paisley delicately wiped her eyes with a faint blush on her cheeks. "Thank you for wanting to find out who hurt my mum."

For once, Motts believed she was seeing Paisley without artifice. She stayed silent, hoping the grieving woman would share more. River appeared to be keeping Louis busy elsewhere in the cottage; she heard their muffled voices.

"Mum wanted more from me." Paisley rested

against the doorframe. "She didn't approve of Louis. He didn't take life seriously enough for her. Now he's all I have."

"How are things going at the brewery between the two of you?" Motts asked after Paisley drifted into a morose silence. "Are you getting on well together?"

"Of course we are." Louis came up behind them. He placed a possessive hand on Paisley's arm. "The police are here. They want everyone outside."

Detective Inspector Rebecca Yuen stood chatting with Hughie on the pavement outside the cottage. Motts elbowed River, who chuckled at the sight. She had no doubts he'd be teasing the poor constable about his crush later.

They were separated to give their statements to Hughie while the inspector went inside the cottage. Motts sat on the wall around the front garden, trying to listen to what Louis had to say. She didn't trust him.

"Fancy meeting you here." Hughie offered a smile when it was finally Motts's turn for questions. "Can you tell me what happened?"

Motts rubbed her arms from a sudden chill; clouds had moved in, and the temperature had begun to drop. "Nothing terribly exciting, to be fair.

We came over to check out Petunia's cottage. Everything was clean. Clinically clean, carefully contained. I went to check out the bedroom only to see someone had wrecked the place."

"Does anything else stand out?"

"Paisley mentioned Ernest Herring had been in the cottage yesterday. He took a box away with him." Motts eased her hands into her sleeves to warm her fingers up. "Have you asked the enchanting detective inspector out yet?"

"Motts." Hughie closed his notebook and slipped it into his pocket. "Why don't you have River take you home? I imagine the cottage is going to be closed off again."

"Fine, fine. Thanks, Hughie." Motts hopped off the wall, deciding to leave Paisley and Louis to their conversation. She jogged across the road and got into the blissful warmth of River's car. "Bit chilly for October."

"Why don't we stop by the café? Get some tea?"

"I'd rather go home." She wanted time to process their morning. Cactus would probably be cold with the change of weather. "I need some space to think."

And decide how to eliminate suspects from our list.

CHAPTER SEVENTEEN

"FUNERALS ARE NEVER AN ENJOYABLE EXPERIENCE." Motts stood in front of the bathroom mirror, attempting to bully one strand of hair into cooperating. "No one goes to enjoy themselves. It's a crowd. An emotional throng."

Her reflection had no response. Cactus also remained unmoved by her early morning angst. Typical. He lounged across her bed, lazily batting at a paper ball.

"Don't get soggy paper on the duvet," Motts warned. Cactus peered over at her before going back to playing. "Want to go to the funeral with me? My emotional support feline?"

Meow.

"It's possible they wouldn't appreciate your

glorious presence." Motts checked the clock on her bedside for the tenth time. "River's late. I don't fancy riding my Vespa to a funeral."

As if on cue, the doorbell rang several times. Motts double-checked Cactus's food and water dishes were appropriately filled. She grabbed her bag and a cardigan, heading out the door to where River waited.

"I brought doughnuts and coffee."

"You're my favourite cousin." Motts needed the sugary fortification to get her through the morning. "My only cousin. Still my fave."

"Hughie's got a date."

"And you're not going to ruin it for him." Motts was pleased to hear their loveable constable had asked his crush out. "Did Hughie share anything else with you?"

"The box Ernest Herring took supposedly had his stuff—according to him, of course. He also claimed the bedroom was fine when he visited the cottage." River handed the doughnut box to Motts while he started the car. "If he's telling the truth, someone else went into the cottage."

"Who? And why?" Motts lifted the lid to inspect the selection. River had gone to one of the fancier doughnut shops in Looe. She was torn between a

Jaffa Cake one and a honeycomb one. "Did he say if they noticed any damage to the cottage? Any proof someone broke into it?"

"Nope. I certainly didn't see any broken glass or signs of a door being forced when we were there." River paused at the bottom of the lane. "Are you going to eat a doughnut or stare at them for the entire trip?"

"Doughnut delights deliciously." She picked the Jaffa Cake one, choosing to eat the bits of biscuit off the top first. "We could stay in your car with these and the coffee, watch who shows up at the funeral without going inside."

"You'll never know who shows up to the service if you hide." He did have a point. "I'll be by your side the whole time. It'll be fine."

Fine, in retrospect, had been wishful thinking. Their drive to Looe was the best part of the morning. Delectable pastries, strong coffee, and casual chatter between cousins. Motts enjoyed herself immensely.

Finding a parking space hadn't been easy. River managed to find one down the street from the church. They made the walk up; almost everyone was already inside.

They could hear raised voices coming from the foyer. River led her inside. Motts immediately recognised Louis, who appeared to be in an argument with an older man.

River caught her by the hand to drag her behind a pillar. "That's Louis's father."

"Ah," Motts murmured. "Why in the world would they be shouting at each other at a funeral service?"

Before they could figure the answer out, the parish priest interrupted the argument. Motts frowned in disappointment. She'd hoped to hear a little of it.

While Mr Banks and the priest talked, Louis stormed away. Motts jotted down what happened in her notebook. Odd behaviour wasn't criminal, but all the small details often added up to murder.

Funerals find family fully fragmented.

Nothing stood out about the service itself. Songs were sung, scriptures read, and stories told. Paisley offered an emotional tribute to her mum.

Motts had to wipe a few tears away with the sleeve of her cardigan. Emotions were so strange. Someone across the way caught her attention. "River?"

He bent toward her, keeping his voice low when his mum clucked her tongue at him. "Yeah?"

"Check out Ernest Herring." She nodded her

head towards Petunia's supposedly grieving fiancé. "I know everyone deals with death differently, but...."

"He's more stone-faced than most. I'd be devastated if anything happened to Nish." River glanced behind them. "Louis finished his tantrum. Surprised he's not hovering over Paisley."

"Me too." Motts lowered her voice even further when Auntie Lily glanced her way. "Think something is going on with them?"

"I'm not sure. I don't recall Paisley being so... subdued." River shrugged. "Grief affects everyone differently, though, like you said."

Despite another nudge from her aunt, Motts struggled to settle down. The service dragged on once the parish priest got up to speak. She wished they'd chosen to sit closer to an exit.

"I spy with my little eye something beginning with the letter *d*," River whispered.

"*River*."

"Not that. Honestly. Such a naughty thought in a church."

Motts flicked her cousin on his leg and stared at him in confusion. "Oh, joke. Right."

"Yes." River's face went through all sorts of contortions while he tried not to laugh. "Well, I spy someone beginning with *d*."

Casting a glance around the church, Motts spied Dempsey standing beside the two Polperro detectives. She wondered when he'd arrived in Cornwall. He'd probably stayed with Hughie again.

As the service wrapped up, Motts watched Louis move over to offer comfort to a quietly weeping Paisley. They sat stiffly on the bench, obviously uncomfortable. Paisley steadfastly refused to glance anywhere but at the photo of her mum at the front of the church.

Am I reading too much into body language? Probably. I'm pants at it. Why am I trying?

"Do you want to go up and pay your respects?" her aunt asked once the service ended. "Or perhaps River should take you outside?"

"I can manage." Motts wanted River to stay in the church in case something happened. She also wasn't a toddler who required an escort. "I'll get some air."

Ducking through groups of people, Motts managed to step into the cool breeze and slight mist. She tilted her head up, enjoying the mild drizzle. The door squeaked open behind her, closing a second later with a thud.

"Small crowd for a funeral."

"There would be." Motts kept her eyes closed,

enjoying the cool mist. Dempsey obviously hadn't spent loads of time in small villages. "There'll be double the crowd at the 'celebration of life' at the brewery."

"Free food and beer." Dempsey stepped up beside her. "I heard about the fruit attack."

"I'm aware. I texted you. It wasn't only fruit." Motts suddenly dropped her head down, wrapping her cardigan around herself more tightly, a sudden chill going straight through her. "I haven't had any other incidents since then."

Dempsey eased off his overcoat and dropped it across her shoulders. "Why don't we chat on the way to the brewery?" He led her over to his vehicle. She climbed into the seat, breathing a sigh of relief when he turned on the heat to full whack. The sudden quiet after the loud hum of the funeral felt even better than being warm.

"Do you want to chat? Or have quiet time on the drive?" Dempsey left the decision to Motts, who appreciated his thoughtfulness greatly.

"Do you know if they found out how Petunia died?" Motts wasn't ready to talk about the bracelet, Jenny, or the pale blue car following her around. She thought she'd seen the vehicle a few more times since the first. "Did she drown?"

Dempsey shook his head and chuckled. "I knew you couldn't resist the mystery. As it happens, DI Ash wanted my thoughts on the case and shared some of the details with me."

"And?"

"Petunia suffered blunt force trauma to the head. The actual cause of death was drowning." Dempsey eased his vehicle out of the car park and onto the road. "They found liquid in her lungs."

"How awful." Motts tried not to think about being trapped inside a barrel, slowly dying with no hope of escape. "What kind of a monster does that?"

"Someone who's quite angry." Dempsey made the understatement of the year. "I believe she was drowned before going into the barrel."

"Small mercies."

The rest of the drive was spent in silence. Motts hunkered down in Dempsey's coat, trying to organise her thoughts further. If Petunia had been drowned, did it mean someone stronger had been involved?

Was Paisley off the hook?

Or had she relied on Louis for the heavy lifting?

In her heart, Motts didn't believe Paisley had been involved in her mother's death. She'd acted oddly, sure. Louis was another matter, though; he definitely had a motive and the strength to do it.

"Here we are." Dempsey drew her out of her thoughts as he parked at the brewery. "Already quite a few here."

"Told you." Motts wasn't surprised. She imagined there would be loads from the village showing up. "It's going to be a long morning."

Thirty minutes after they arrived, everyone had shown up for a party. Chairs had been brought into the open space in the brewhouse. Everyone sat around, drinking and chatting about Petunia's life.

It was a lot. Some appeared genuinely sad. Others had definitely come for drinks and gossip— not that she blamed them.

As people continued sharing memories, Motts strolled away from the group toward the rows of barrels. She breathed in deeply, counting to five. It was definitely time to go home.

She'd had enough of socialising.

"Hello?" Motts heard a cough nearby. She walked by several rows, trying to find the person. "Is someone there?"

A crack echoing from further down the stack was the only answer. Motts spun around in time to find a row of barrels cascading toward her. Someone had caused the entire shelf to tilt in her direction, sending them falling like dominoes.

Bugger.

I should've stayed at home.

Diving away from the oncoming stampede, Motts crushed herself between two empty units. Broken barrel chunks and beer spewed forth at an alarming rate. She climbed up onto one of the shelves, attempting to escape the tidal wave of malty liquid.

Running footsteps caught her attention off to one side. Motts leaned forward and spotted a man ducking between another set of shelves. He was out the emergency exit in a second, giving her barely a glimpse of a dark grey jacket.

"Motts?"

"Up here." Motts waved to Dempsey, who'd sloshed through the spilt beer with the Polperro police, River, and her uncle close behind. She caught Hughie's attention, gesturing to her left. "He went through the emergency exit."

"Did he?" Hughie was gone in a flash.

"You saw who did this?" Dempsey continued picking his way toward her.

"I'd wager it was him." Motts gave a brief description of his clothes, watching as Detective Inspector Yuen jotted it down on a notebook. She hadn't caught a glimpse of his face, unfortunately.

"We were the only people on this side of the warehouse."

I will find time to panic later.

I am fine.

I'm okay. I am okay. I'm okay.

I am okay.

No matter how many repetitions, Motts didn't believe herself. She didn't know how to get down without injury. *I'll live here forever on this shelf in a brewery.*

"Let's get you off the shelf." Dempsey climbed over the wreckage of barrels. "Whoever did this wouldn't stick around, not with so many witnesses."

With a hand from Dempsey and River, Motts made it to dry land. Her shoes, socks, and trousers were soaked through from the beer. She trembled as cold and delayed panic sank into her bones.

"Were you injured? Young Pineapple?" Her uncle appeared with a blanket over one arm. He flicked it out to wrap around her. "Your auntie had this in her handbag."

"Of course she did." River snickered. He calmed a little when his dad glared at him. "Mum carries everything needed for an apocalypse in her purse."

With her hands buried in the soft fleece, Motts wilted into her uncle's hug. He walked her through the curious onlookers and outside. She shivered despite the warmth from the blanket.

"Why don't we get you to your cottage and your Cactus?" Her uncle stopped in the car park when Hughie jogged over to them. "Did you find anything, young man?"

"You're not a cop." Motts nudged her uncle in the side, despite her curiosity. "Uncle Tomato."

"I've known the lad since he stumbled around with his thumb in his mouth." Her uncle refused to be cowed by the massive Hughie, who grinned. "He wasn't always a giant."

"I didn't find anyone out here." Hughie ignored the chuckling from her uncle. "Do we need to call the ambulance?"

"Not a scratch on me," Motts assured everyone. She couldn't quite stop herself from shivering. "Could someone give me a lift home?"

"Come on. We'll swing by the café to get something warm for you." River caught her hand, pulling her away from her uncle. She tripped over the end of the blanket but didn't fall. "If we hurry, they'll be too distracted to ask you more questions."

And they were.

"Are you okay?" River kept glancing over at her while he drove. "You're shaking."

"I'm cold. Don't pester me." Motts wanted to be in her cottage with no sound other than a purring Cactus and a crackling fireplace. "Home, River. Not the café."

Giving her one last worried look, River nodded his head. The ride went on for what felt like hours. Motts wanted to be home.

It was a mantra in her head. She repeated it over and over until River eased his vehicle up the lane. She all but ran inside, shutting the door and leaning against it.

I'll apologise later. River would understand. She hoped.

Getting a fire going took longer than expected. Motts's fingers didn't want to cooperate. She shook out her hands a few times and tried again.

Finally.

Motts held her hands out, enjoying the building warmth. Nothing drove away the cold like a fire or a hot bath. She'd have one of those later.

Meow.

She gathered Cactus up into her arms, rubbing her nose against his peach fuzz. "What a day I've had."

CHAPTER EIGHTEEN

Motts woke up the following day to a shed-load of text messages. She'd shut off her phone before crawling into bed. The uninterrupted peace had done wonders for her. "Why don't we stroll around the garden this morning, eh?"

With Cactus on her heels, Motts carried her second mug of tea into the garden. She let the cardigan-wearing cat prance around while she replied to messages. None of them were urgent; most simply wanted to make sure she was okay.

She was. Mostly. The accident at the brewery hadn't left a mark on her. Her hands had stopped trembling.

All good things.

While sipping her tea, Motts considered the

events of the previous day. She no longer believed Paisley was involved in her mother's death. Louis remained on the list.

One other question lingered for her. Why had someone tried to hurt her with the barrels of beer? It had to be a pointed attack.

No one else had been even close to Motts at the time. Maybe someone wanted to damage the beer with her, an innocent bystander, caught up in the wreckage. She didn't think so.

The killer had obviously noticed her investigation. The barrels had been a warning or an attempted murder. She'd had more than enough time to escape.

Meow.

"You're right. I'm not going to solve anything sitting here and worrying over what might have been." Motts reached out to pat Cactus's head when he paused in his exploration. "Are you enjoying yourself?"

"Knock, knock," her granddad called out from the other side of the garden gate. "Can I come in?"

"What would you do if I said no?"

"Take the scones and leave?"

"You're in luck. Scones are the secret password." Motts watched him reach over to unlock the gate and come inside. "What did you bring?"

"Your gran made these. My Martha. Lovely woman, she is." He showed her a familiar basket filled to the brim. "Honey and apricot scones, apparently. She included a homemade jam as well."

Motts sat up on the lounge chair, watching as Cactus went over to greet their visitor. "I'd never turn down Gran's cooking."

"How are you doing, poppet?" Her granddad went over to peek into the greenhouse section of the shed. "See, these are doing well. You'll have a lovely time with these through the winter."

"I'm keeping a close eye on them." Motts had gotten a selection of vegetables in her little greenhouse. It was her first attempt at a winter garden, so her granddad had helped her pick more hardy ones to start with, like leeks, peas, and endives plus a few herbs. "I think most of them will survive well."

"Good." He came over to stand beside her. "Why don't we head inside? You can tell me all about your adventure over tea and scones."

"And how many scones have you already had?" Motts laughed when he pretended to sulk. Her granddad always found a way to lift her mood. "Don't worry. I won't tell Gran."

"How about you, young man?" He reached out to greet Cactus, who purred contentedly at the attention. "I haven't forgotten about you. There's something special in the basket for you as well."

Over a warm cup of tea and several scones slathered with jam, Motts went through the chaos of the funeral. She didn't know how she'd escaped without a scratch. Her granddad listened without interjecting his thoughts; he was good at that.

He leaned forward to pat her hand gently. "Be careful, poppet. We've only got one of you."

"Well, yes, because I don't have a clone." Motts ate the last bite of scone. They'd gone through the entire batch between them. "I try to be careful. Other people just don't cooperate with my attempts."

With a wry grin and another pat to her hand, her granddad said his goodbyes. He took the empty basket with him. Motts sat in her kitchen, trying to decide what to do next with her investigation.

If Paisley is off my suspect list, who do I focus on next? Louis? Ernest, with his odd behaviour at the funeral? Or the perpetually angry Heath?

Is it the daughter's boyfriend? The fiancé? Or the co-worker?

Or none of the above, and I'm completely off base.

It wouldn't be the first time.

Marnie!

It occurred to Motts that she'd intended to speak with Marnie and forgotten. She decided to walk down to the village. Fresh air always made her feel better, and breakfast with her granddad had already gone a long way into brushing off the drama of the previous day.

"Morning." Marnie greeted when Motts pushed the door open into the bridal shop. "Perry mentioned the barrel accident yesterday. Were you hurt? Should you be up and about?"

"I'm fine. Less of an accident, more of an incident." Motts frowned for a second. "Purposeful incident. You know what I meant."

Waving her over to the consultation table in the corner of the room, Marnie grabbed a tin of biscuits and began heating up the kettle for tea. She sat across from Motts, who'd gotten distracted by a fabric swatch book. It was new, and one of the patterns caught her eye; it would make for an exciting quilling project.

"Did you see who knocked the barrels over?"

"Only a glimpse of their coat." Motts found the only bourbon biscuit left in the tin and grabbed it. "I didn't recognise them. Whoever did this knew enough about the brewery to release the barrels in a way they'd fall like dominos."

"It might've been a lucky break for them."

"Maybe." Motts didn't think so, though.

From helping out at the Chen-Mottley brewery, Motts knew a little about the way barrels were stacked. She'd bet her life someone had known which post to break to cause them to cascade as they had. It certainly wasn't an accident.

Not that she'd ever believed it had been.

It frustrated her greatly to not have seen his face. Odds were they'd be able to identify Petunia's killer if she had. *I should ask Paisley about CCTV footage from inside the brewery. Maybe we can figure out who wasn't with the crowd of mourners.*

"You've thought of something." Marnie nibbled on a custard cream, dunking it briefly into her tea. "Go on, what is it?"

"If the barrels falling was caused by the killer, they were at the funeral." Motts dug around for another biscuit from the tin. "So, maybe cameras at the brewery either spotted the person or at least can tell us who wasn't with the rest of those gathered to celebrate Petunia's life."

"Oh, you are a clever sausage, aren't you?"

"I'm not a sausage. I'm a person," Motts countered. She scowled at the chuckling Marnie. "Figure of speech?"

"Yes, love." Marnie finished up her second biscuit. "It's a lovely day for a ride to Looe."

"Isn't it, though?" She decided to send a text to Paisley on the off-chance they could meet at the brewery. "I'm going to have a busy morning."

"Off you go, then." Marnie ushered her out of the bridal shop, handing a little packet of biscuits to her. "Energy for the journey."

Deciding the Griffin twins would only delay her, Motts retraced her way up to her cottage. She paused on the top step, eyeing the familiar pale blue car parked down the lane. When she focused her camera on the vehicle, the driver immediately began reversing.

This is not a coincidence. They're definitely following me.

As Motts continued to film, the vehicle vanished from sight. A few minutes later, Dempsey's Range Rover came up the lane. She waved at him, pressing pause on the video.

Dempsey pulled up beside her and lowered his window. "Hello."

"You couldn't have been two minutes earlier,"

Motts complained. "Did you happen to see a blue car?"

"The Nissan?"

"Pale blue car, no idea the make or model. It's the one stalking me." Motts considered her words. "The car isn't. It can't actively follow anyone."

"Did you get a peek at the driver?" Dempsey went to open his door, stopping when she held her hand up. "Problem?"

"I was on my way to see Paisley. Want to go to the Coastal Port Brewery with me?" Motts didn't believe he'd want her to go by herself. "I'd planned to ride my Vespa over now."

"Continuing your investigation, are you?" Dempsey grinned.

Motts shrugged in response.

"Hop in." Dempsey unlocked the door, waiting for her to climb inside. "You might check your camera feeds and make sure no one's mucked around the cottage."

Her alarm hadn't tripped. Motts checked all the camera feeds and didn't see anything suspicious other than her cat. Cactus had found one of her origami creatures for a new project and tossed the paper around the living room, only to then hunt it down.

Silly feline.

Dempsey leaned across the centre console to see what had her giggling to herself. "Fierce feline."

"Fierce feline frolics funnily." She was relieved to see the stalker hadn't come up to her cottage. "Why sit and watch my home? Why follow me around?"

"Send me the video you took of the car." Dempsey slowly reversed down the lane until he could turn around. He glanced around each side street they passed. "Keep an eye out. I want the vehicle registration number if we can catch a glimpse. Have you seen what you captured on your phone? Maybe you already have it."

"I wonder if anyone connected to Paisley has a pale blue car." Motts wondered aloud. "I can't remember seeing one at the funeral or at the brewery afterwards."

"Perhaps. No harm in asking. I can get the video over to Perry," Dempsey promised. "He won't have as many questions if I'm sending him something."

True.

And Perry might give Dempsey more details than he'd give me.

On the trip to the brewery, Motts checked out the short video on her phone. It wasn't clear enough, at least on the small screen, to get the vehicle registration. She made sure to send a copy over to Dempsey.

Maybe the police could find a way to zoom in where her phone couldn't.

"What are you expecting from Paisley?" Dempsey asked after she'd pocketed her phone.

"Not sure. She was eager for me to come over when I messaged her, though." Motts didn't know what to expect with Paisley's constantly changing moods. "Surprisingly so."

They arrived at the brewery quickly, having missed much of the morning traffic. Paisley had already made it out of the building by the time they'd parked. Motts didn't know what to make of her desperate enthusiasm.

"I'm so glad you're here." Paisley grabbed her hand desperately, keeping her voice barely above a whisper. "Louis's dealing with the mess leftover in the brewery. We have some time to ourselves."

"Okay." Motts let herself be led along the familiar path to what had been Petunia's office. "Why are we whispering?"

Paisley's gaze darted from Motts to Dempsey to the closed office door. "Louis might've killed my mum."

Silence didn't usually feel tangible, Motts thought in the wake of Paisley's confession. She could practically touch the quiet.

"I'll keep an eye out for Louis." Dempsey stepped out of the office, shutting the door behind him.

The silence continued for several minutes. Paisley didn't seem to be ready to speak. She arranged and rearranged the stacks of brewery pamphlets on the desk.

Waiting wasn't always easy for Motts. She enjoyed the peaceful calm of her cottage. This quiet was incredibly loud, as if someone was punching her in the eardrums.

Paisley threw the pamphlets with a hiss of frustration. "Video footage of the day Mum died was corrupted."

"What?" Motts asked. "How?"

"One of the detectives told me. They downloaded all the files from the day of her murder. Every one had been corrupted." Paisley dragged a second chair behind the desk for Motts to sit. "I find it odd."

"Very odd." Motts believed suspicious might be a better word. "What about yesterday?"

"I went through each of our cameras. Only one caught a glimpse of something—or someone, rather."

Paisley moved the mouse around to get it working, then clicked play on the video. "None of the face was visible. They actively avoided being caught in a way we could identify them."

They played the CCTV footage five times. Neither woman could identify the figure captured on screen. A silhouette of a male figure in a coat. Nothing helpful by any stretch of the imagination.

"I don't remember seeing anyone at the church or brewery with a similar coat." Paisley paused the video before it repeated for the sixth time. "Did you?"

"No." Motts shook her head, leaning in closer as if the distance was the problem. "Why do you think Louis might've hurt your mum?"

Paisley sat back in her chair. She fussed with the pamphlets once again. "He's acted oddly since before Mum passed away. He called me from university the day she went missing, or so I thought."

"But?"

Paisley crumpled one of the pamphlets in her hand. "Ernie came to the gravesite to talk to me. He claimed to have seen Louis on the street outside Mum's cottage the day before. He never said anything about coming to Cornwall."

"Was this why you argued with Ernie?"

She tried to straighten the pamphlet out, eventually giving up and throwing the ruined paper in the bin. "Partly. I thought he'd stolen Mum's belongings. Now I'm not so sure."

"Have you spoken with the detectives about any of this?"

"I've no proof of anything." Paisley shifted her chair around to face Motts. "You could help. Mikey said. He said you'd solved his nan's murder. I know I asked you to find her for me. And you did. Can't you help figure out if Louis is guilty?"

"Maybe." Motts refused to make any promises. She had no idea who'd murdered Petunia or how to find the truth. "The police likely have a better chance at solving the mystery."

"But you will try, won't you?"

"I'll do my best."

CHAPTER NINETEEN

"What now?" Dempsey asked. They stood outside the brewery. He'd readily followed her out when she'd wrapped up her conversation with Paisley. "Any thoughts?"

"I want to see the shed again." Motts didn't know why, but she had to walk the path the killer would've taken with Petunia—or her body, at least. "None of this makes any sense."

"Murder rarely does."

As they made their way around the side of the brewery, Motts summarised her conversation with Paisley. Dempsey found her sudden admission to be suspicious. He had a point.

Why had she decided to break from Louis now?

What wasn't Paisley sharing with them?

"You've gone all quiet," Dempsey asked when she'd stood still for several minutes, staring at the back of the building. "What are you seeing?"

"The happy couple."

"We're definitely being observed. I feel like a specimen under a microscope." Dempsey waved cheerfully at the couple, who instantly moved out of sight, blinds dropping down to obscure the window. "Something I said?"

"You are without a doubt the oddest police detective I've ever met in person." Motts continued toward the shed with their audience gone. "Do you think Petunia was killed here or in her office, then carried to the barrel?"

"With no cameras pointed this direction, the smartest thing would've been to bring her to the shed under false pretences." Dempsey leaned against the side of the shed. He gestured down the path in the grass. "The killer couldn't have counted on the CCTV files being corrupted. It's an old system, so I'm not surprised, but they wouldn't have known. My guess is they brought her out of the brewery, had her walking in front of them, knocked her out, and then drowned her."

"Your guess is both specific and disturbing." Motts tried not to visualise the graphic details of

Petunia's murder. "How difficult would it have been to carry Petunia?"

"Depends on the person doing the lifting."

He had a point. A good one. All of those she considered to be potential suspects would've physically been capable of lifting Petunia up.

Paisley? Not so much.

A thorough glance around the front of the shed showed nothing had changed since her last visit. Motts hadn't expected any. *What am I hoping to find?*

"I need a different perspective." Motts found a clear spot near the shed and sat down on a soft patch of grass. She rested her hands behind her, leaning back to take in the view from the ground level. Something occurred to her almost immediately. "Anyone at the brewery could've seen the killer. There are employees. How did they lead her out back and murder her with no one observing anything?"

"The coroner wasn't able to give us an exact time of death." Dempsey stretched out on the grass beside her. "Brine likely messed with the decomposition."

"Pickled." Motts tried not to laugh. She did. "I am a horrible person."

"You're human. A little macabre humour gets all of us at times." Dempsey offered a reassuring smile.

"Life enjoys messing with our heads every once in a while."

"Have DI Ash or Yuen shared anything else about the case?"

Dempsey shook his head, picking at a blade of grass and using it to whistle. "I'm loath to inject myself too much into the official investigation. Detective inspectors can be territorial at the best of times."

"Loath." Motts repeated the word a few times to herself. "You genuinely have the best words."

"I do my best."

It was a lovely day to sit out in the grass. Motts could almost forget why they'd come out to the brewery. The shed was a stark reminder.

Someone had been murdered here.

"Our audience has returned." Dempsey flicked a piece of grass at her to get her attention.

Motts watched as Paisley and Louis reappeared in the office window. Unlike the previous time, they were deep in conversation and focused on each other. It was a very animated chat, based on the arm-waving both of them were doing.

"Interesting." Dempsey stood up after watching Paisley storm out of view. "We should catch up with her."

"Why?"

"Emotionally distraught people often share more than they intend." Dempsey reached down to help her to her feet. "She's also likely to be more brutally honest about Louis than a loyal partner might otherwise be."

Rushing to the car park, they found Paisley by her vehicle. She'd collapsed against her car. Motts could see tears still streaming down her face.

What had happened?

"Paisley?" Motts hesitantly reached out to touch her arm. "Are you all right?"

"He's sacked me." Paisley bit the words out, brushing angrily at the tears on her cheeks. "He actually sacked me."

"Louis sacked you? His girlfriend?" Motts couldn't possibly have heard Paisley right. "Can he do that? Wouldn't his parents be the ones in charge of hiring and firing?"

"He suggested we might want to take some time to ourselves. He broke up with me. And then he sacked me." Paisley wilted against her vehicle. "What am I going to do?"

"I'd be grateful he broke up with you. He's obviously a complete git. He's saved you a lot of heartache later on if you'd gotten married." Motts glanced over at Dempsey, who'd obviously gotten something stuck in his throat from all the coughing. "Do you need some water? What?"

Maybe I should've been more comforting?

I'd find that thought comforting.

Who wants to be stuck for life with a grubby little worm like Louis obviously is?

Despite Dempsey's earlier claims, Paisley ran out of words quickly. She gave a muted goodbye, got in her car, and sped off. Motts could only stare after her, waving.

"So, Louis sacked Heath Miller, essentially setting himself up as the brewmaster. He waits until they've reorganised the office, then gets rid of his girlfriend as well." Dempsey scratched his jaw, staring at the brewery. "He's certainly gone to the top of my list."

"And mine, as well," Motts readily agreed.

"How about I drop you off at Griffin Brews?" Dempsey got his vehicle started, reversing and heading away from the brewery. "I've got to see a man about a dog."

"That phrase never makes sense. You don't even want a dog, do you?"

"More of a cat person," Dempsey admitted.

"How about... I've a detective inspector to see about a potentially criminal lubberwort."

"Now you're doing it to make fun of me. Is lubberwort even a word?"

"Mythical vegetable from ye olden days." Dempsey grinned when she scowled at him. "I might have a better chance of getting information out of your local police."

Motts made a mental note to do an internet search for lubberwort. "I've a feeling you could get their entire life story if you put in a little effort."

"I've a kind face."

"It's something." Motts stared at his profile for several seconds before turning back to staring out the window. "What makes a face kind?"

"The dimples and carefully managed salt-and-pepper beard?"

"Handsome and kind aren't the same thing." Motts grabbed her reusable water bottle from her backpack to have a drink.

"You think I'm handsome?"

"You're aesthetically pleasing." Motts sank into silence in the vehicle while Dempsey chuckled to himself for the rest of the drive to Polperro.

After being dropped off, Motts headed into the

café. The morning rush was over, and the lunch crowd had yet to start. She sat at one of the tables closest to the counter, filling Vina in on her discoveries.

"What an actual snake of a man." Vina shook her head, sending her long ponytail flying. "Dumped and sacked the same day. Poor Paisley. She's better off without him, though. Imagine being married, having all these joint things, and then finding out he's a lying—"

"Watch your language."

"Sorry, Amma." Vina rolled her eyes at Motts's snicker. "Well, we know who killed Petunia now. Obviously."

"Maybe." Motts didn't think being a massive prat equalled murderer. "He definitely had a motive if he wanted control of the brewery. Though, if he did, why not fire Petunia like he did with Heath and Paisley?"

"Maybe his parents wouldn't have gone for it." Vina made an excellent point.

"Oi. Are you finished with your gossip break? We've got loads of stuff to bring out of the kitchen." Nish nudged Vina on his way to clear the table off behind them. "Don't be lazy because Motts is here."

"Rude." Vina stuck her tongue out at her brother.

"And highly unnecessary, since I'm supporting Mottsy in her time of need."

"You're gossiping with Mottsy," Nish corrected.

"It's about Louis."

"Oh?" Nish immediately came over to drop into the spare seat across from his sister. "What's he done now?"

"Tossed Paisley out on her ear—both professionally and personally," Vina answered for Motts. "They've barely buried Petunia. He's sacked Heath and Paisley, setting himself up as the sole management of his family business."

"Hasn't he, though?" Nish jumped up when Caden came out of the kitchen with a giant tray. "Right. Back to work with us."

"You'd never guess we were all grown up." Vina laughed. "He's still playing the good son, making sure he's working harder than anyone else."

"Maybe he's passionate about working at the café." Motts eyed Vina, who finally went back to work with a dramatic huff. "I wouldn't say we're *all* grown up."

"Rude."

CHAPTER TWENTY

MOTTS WOKE UP THE FOLLOWING MORNING TO A persistent paw poking at the side of her head and a yowling in her ear. "Cactus? What's wrong?"

Cactus continued to make a fuss until Motts dragged herself out from under the blankets. She grabbed the glass of water from the bedside table, taking a long drink while staring out into the garden. He pawed at the window.

What in the world is wrong with my garden?

The cup slipped from Motts's fingers, sending shards of glass and water flying across the floor. *Bugger.* She stretched out to grab her shoes to hopefully avoid completely shredding her feet. Cactus complained when she locked him in the bathroom for safety.

After cleaning everything up, Motts stumbled downstairs and out the back door. There were dead plants through her garden. She was glad Cactus had been safely locked up in the cottage.

Was it poison?

She was devastated about the state of her lovely garden. There were streaks of some sort of liquid across the rows. It seemed as though someone had sprayed her plants down from over the fence.

What do I do? Is this criminal? Should I call the police?

Plant police politely parade.

Why would someone do this?

Taking her phone from her dressing gown pocket, Motts sent a message to her group chat. She didn't feel up to making an actual call. An icon at the top of the screen caught her attention.

The security system app had noticed an issue with one of her exterior cameras. Motts had slept through the alert. She peered around, eventually catching sight of the empty spot where one had once been attached to the cottage.

Someone had knocked the camera off the house. How had it not woken her up? She regretted falling asleep with her noise-cancelling headphones. Perhaps they'd worked a little too well.

"Motts?"

She wasn't surprised Hughie had been the first person to show up. He lived just down the lane. "Come through the gate."

"Where's Cactus?" Hughie asked while taking in the damage. "Have you touched anything?"

"I touched the door handle." Motts ignored the onslaught of buzzing from her phone. "Cactus is safely ensconced upstairs. Why would someone do this? What even is it?"

"My guess would be some form of weed killer." Hughie pulled on a pair of gloves, then stepped over the single healthy row of plants to crouch down next to one of the dead ones. "Smells like it as well."

"Weed killer?" Motts leaned against the cottage. "We'll have to rip everything out, won't we? How long will the poison stay in the soil? Doesn't it start to break down at some point?"

"Depends on what's been used. It could be a few weeks or months. It might never fully break down." Hughie continued inspecting the damaged plants. "If necessary, I can build raised beds for you. I'd bet your granddad has some ideas as well. We can haul in clean soil, get you some new seeds, and have it all as good as new."

Motts could only shrug in response. She struggled to do anything beyond staring at what had been her beautiful herbs, vegetables, and fruits. "Cactus always runs out into the garden in the mornings. Could this have killed him like it did the plants?"

Before Hughie could answer, the chaotic trio from her group chat came clattering through the cottage. River had clearly used his spare key again. Motts almost regretted giving it to him.

"Stop." Hughie got to his feet. His command caused her three best friends to skid to a halt. "This is a crime scene. I don't want your footprints mucking our chance of identifying who did this."

"Sorry, Hughie." Nish grabbed River by the back of his jacket to keep him from stumbling out the door. "What happened?"

"Mottsy?" Vina sidled up to her, placing an arm around her shoulders. "Why don't you come inside? Let's get you dressed. Nish can whip something up for breakfast while Hughie does his investigation."

Motts allowed herself to be led upstairs. She closed the door and released Cactus from his bathroom prison. He immediately hopped up on the bed, rolling around on the duvet.

Motts fell back beside him, covering her face with a pillow and screaming into it for several seconds. "I'm so angry."

"Good. You should be." Vina lifted the pillow away from her face once Motts finished shouting. "Feel any better?"

"Not really." Motts sniffed. She sat up, clutching the pillow like a teddy. "I love my plants."

"I'm aware."

"They ruined my garden."

"Brilliant thing about plants? You can get more of them." Vina began putting an outfit together for Motts. She found her favourite cardigan, a loose T-shirt, and her most comfortable corduroy dungarees. "I've got your most comfy clothes."

"I'm still angry." Motts rested her chin on the pillow.

"Nothing wrong with being justifiably upset." Vina laid out her outfit on the bed. "I'm running a bath. You can wash up, get dressed, and come downstairs whenever you're ready."

"And then?"

"We find whoever ruined your leafy babies," Vina promised. She grabbed Motts by the wrist and bustled her toward the bathroom. "Come on. I'll take Cactus downstairs with me while you relax."

The soak in the tub did wonders for Motts's mood. She dressed quickly, refusing to stare out the window. Breakfast would hopefully get her mind up and running.

The sound hit her on the way down the stairs.

There were loads more people in the cottage. They'd multiplied. The entire Griffin clan, minus Nish, had crowded into the kitchen along with her gran and auntie Lily. River, her granddad, uncle, and Nish appeared to be in the garden with the police.

The police had also multiplied. Hughie had been joined by the Polperro detectives and Dempsey. Her cottage was far too small for the number of people.

Cactus had taken up his spot by the window, watching the activity outside. Motts would have to keep an eye on him to make sure he didn't sneak out into the garden. An empty bowl sat next to him; someone had already gotten his breakfast together.

"Oh, there you are, poppet." Her gran came over to hug her tightly. "Now, we've got breakfast. And then we're all going to sort out your garden for you."

"Breakfast first." Vina had a plate in one hand and caught Motts's arm in the other. "You'll thank me later."

"What?"

"We'll be right back," Vina yelled to her parents before dragging Motts out the front door and over to the bench in front of the cottage. "We can sit out here and have breakfast. You know they'll just stare at you while you eat otherwise."

Motts sipped the tea. Her gran had definitely made it, based on the sweetness. "Will anyone notice if we never go inside again?"

"Eventually." Vina tapped the plate on the bench between them. "You should eat."

"Mum would take this as yet another sign moving here was a terrible idea." Motts considered the variety of breakfast options, opting for her favourite lemon curd on toast. "She'd insist I return to London."

"But?"

"I've a cottage filled to the brim with loud, lovely people who care about me." She smiled around her bite of toast. "Why would I ever want to leave?"

"You—"

"Vina? Can you go get the detectives? Please?" Motts cut her off sharply. Her full attention was taken by the car she'd spotted down the lane. It was partially hidden behind the line of other vehicles leading up to her cottage. "Now, Vina, hurry."

Walking partially down the lane, Motts had a sense of déjà vu. She had barely gotten her phone out before the person reversed down the road.

Figures. The three police officers joined her several seconds later.

"It's already gone." Motts pointed in the general direction of the village. "Maybe we should put a camera on the corner leading up here?"

"What an excellent idea." Hughie stepped up behind her. "I'll see about getting one installed."

"I've an idea." Dempsey motioned for her to follow him back to the cottage. "Here's what we should do."

"Get rid of the horde invading my cottage?" Motts suggested. "I'll never get anything accomplished with all of them hovering over me."

Hughie snorted with laughter behind them. "She might be right."

"Aren't there regulations about capacity?" Motts figured there had to be a limit for how many well-meaning people could cram into her little cottage.

"I'm not telling them to get out of your cottage." Hughie held up his hands in surrender.

"Methinks Hughie is afraid of my gran."

"I've a healthy respect for all the Mottley women," Hughie countered.

Stepping into the cottage, Motts found her quiet space filled with raised voices. She shifted back and bumped into Dempsey, who placed a hand on her shoulder. This was why Motts preferred to control the number of people in her home.

In the end, Motts's granddad took charge of the situation. He managed to skilfully charm all but her gran and the police into leaving. He was impressively adept at crowd control.

"Do I want to know what got everyone arguing?" Motts sat at the kitchen table with her gran.

"Whether or not to tell your parents."

Motts dropped her head into her hands with a groan. "Please tell me you haven't?"

"I'm firmly in the camp of those who believe that as a grown adult, you are in charge of who knows details about your life. Should you call your dad?" She reached over to gently ease Motts's hands away from her face. "Maybe."

"He'll only tell Mum." Motts could imagine her mother's reaction to everything happening in Polperro.

"Yes, well, our Dale was never a strong sort of character." Her gran patted her cheeks gently, then leaned back in the chair. "He loves you to pieces, though, poppet."

Her gran was right. It didn't always comfort her to know. Motts often wished her dad stood up to her mum more often.

Heading outside for some fresh air, Motts found the detectives inspecting what appeared to be one of her cameras. She went over to see what they'd discovered. Inspector Yuen tilted it for her to get a closer look.

"Someone shot it from quite a distance."

Motts eyed the hole in the lens. "They shot it? So there's probably no video of who wrecked my garden."

Why would Petunia's killer go to these lengths? Is this even related? Maybe Dempsey's right about this all being related to Jenny's murder.

Once the police had left, Motts retreated to the cottage. They'd managed to clean up much of the debris. She'd work on digging up the plants and soil with her granddad later; they had to develop a plan first.

Sitting at the kitchen table with her granddad and Hughie, Motts opened her sketchbook to a fresh page. She grabbed several pens as well. They were trying to figure out the best way to restore her beloved garden.

"I vote for raised beds. We can clear out everything and start over." Hughie drew a loose outline of the garden, demonstrating how things could look. "Cactus might enjoy it as an obstacle course."

"I'll think about it." Motts thought Hughie made it seem like such an easy decision. "I've no idea what to do with any of it. I've lost most of the plants aside from what was in the greenhouse."

"Why don't we leave you to consider all your options, poppet?" Her granddad stared pointedly at Hughie until he hopped to his feet. "Good lad."

Motts looked all the way up at the tall constable who towered over most. "Lad?"

"I've got years on all of you." Her granddad gave her a warm hug. "Lock up behind us, poppet. Don't talk to any strangers."

"Our entire family is strange," Motts retorted. "I could happily not talk to anyone."

"Don't forget your young Cactus." Her granddad squeezed her one last time before heading out with her gran. Hughie lumbered out after them, ducking to avoid the doorframe as he always did. "And don't eat all the scones in one sitting."

"Rude."

With an empty house, Motts hunkered down with Cactus and her laptop. She listened to podcasts, sipped tea, and thought about murder, particularly the recent mystery to fall into her lap. It kept her mind off her garden troubles.

Who had killed Petunia? She had three suspects

to narrow down hopefully into one. They all seemed equally guilty, though.

I should have a chat with Paisley tomorrow. She might have more insights into Louis, at least, if not the other two as well.

I'll text her later.

CHAPTER TWENTY-ONE

Between hot flashes and nightmares, Motts hadn't gotten more than a few hours of sleep. She had a lukewarm bath to rinse off the death-warmed-over feeling. It didn't help.

Since Paisley would be waiting for her at Griffin Brews, Motts decided to head down early. Might as well. Breakfast might help her mind wake up further.

Coffee, clues, croissants.

I wonder if they've made any croissants this morning.

"Hello, hello, hello." Marnie greeted her at the bottom of the steps. "How are things in your cottage?"

"Cactus missed his morning romp in the garden."

Motts tucked her hands into her sleeves. "I didn't trust the soil."

"You'll have to teach Cactus to walk on a leash. You could bring him down into the village." Marnie joined her on the way to the café. "Rumour has it Heath Miller and Louis Banks got into a brawl at the brewery."

"Rumour or eavesdropping on your partner when he's chatting about a case?"

"Officially? Perry never shares his work with me." Marnie grinned unashamedly at her. "As I was saying, rumour has it two people close to Petunia got themselves in a spot of trouble for assaulting each other."

"Paisley's meeting me for breakfast," Motts admitted. She couldn't help laughing at Marnie's sudden interest. "Am I your next source of village gossip?"

"Be sure to pop by the shop later." Marnie veered off from Motts, stepping across the street away from her.

Off to gossip some more.

Nothing ever stays secret in the village for long.

Continuing down the street, Motts noticed Beck chatting with their grandparents outside Griffin Brews. She waved cheerfully at the Ferris trio; Doc and Elyse wandered off with their coffees. Beck jogged over to Motts.

"Hello. You all right?" Beck grinned at her, raising their coffee cup up in a salute. "Heard you had some trouble at your cottage."

"Travails of village life. News hits everyone before you're even sure what happened." Motts wrapped her arms around herself. She regretted not grabbing a jacket to go over her cardigan. "It's gone cold, hasn't it?"

"Yes, yes it has." Beck chuckled. "Most British statement ever. How's your garden?"

"The only small talk I ever get is weather-related." She glanced toward the café where Vina and her mum were both avidly watching through the window. "I'm going to have to redo my entire garden. And maybe find a new best friend."

"Why don't I come over this weekend? We're closed while some work's done in the kitchen. I can bring food and help clear up the mess." Beck paused to sip their coffee, leaning in closer to Motts. "This is me asking you out—well, in—on a date, if you were wondering. Or, if you prefer, we can call it a pre-date, friendly with potential for more."

"I... sure." Motts took a moment to process her thoughts. She wasn't ready to commit to an official outing with anyone. "Friendly. Friendly is good. Maybe more later."

Beck didn't seem bothered at all. They cheerfully saluted Motts again with their coffee cup. "Off to work with me. See you at the weekend."

After watching them walk away, Motts turned toward the café. She rolled her eyes at the sight of Vina and Leena trying to act casual. Their attempt was both tragic and comedic.

"Could you have been any more obvious?" Motts sighed at the unrepentant Vina. "Beck probably thinks you're.... I don't have the right word."

"I can think of a few." Nish squeezed by his sister at the counter. "Paisley's already here. She showed up about ten minutes ago and hid herself at your favourite table. What are you fancying for breakfast?"

To Motts's delight, spiced scones and chocolate ginger croissants were on the menu. She grabbed one of each plus a mug of her favourite latte. Paisley had indeed ensconced herself at the table in the far corner of the café.

Sitting across from her, Motts got her breakfast situated. She had a bite of croissant, unable to resist the buttery, flaky goodness filled with gooey chocolate with a hint of ginger. No matter how many she had, they always tasted as good as the first.

My best friends are pastry geniuses.

"How are you doing?" Motts belatedly remembered a greeting was expected. "Any trouble with Louis?"

"His parents rang me. He didn't have authority to sack either Heath or me." Paisley picked at the remnants of her scone. "I suppose I've a job if I want."

A job with a possible side of death.

"Do you want?"

"Do I want to stare at Louis's smug, handsome face all day?" Paisley crumbled the last bit of her scone.

Right. Is this a yes or a no? I have no clue.

Motts wondered if the Heath-Louis brawl occurred before or after the call. Had the elder Bankses called the former as well? "When did they ring you?"

"Yesterday morning." Paisley shifted uneasily in her chair, glancing toward the small line at the counter. "I went to the brewery and found Heath and Louis fighting. Brutally. They'd bloodied and bruised themselves. Their clothing was torn. I stayed in my car, calling the police for help."

"Were they saying anything?"

"The police?"

"Heath and Louis." Motts finished up the last bite of her croissant.

"I heard shouting about money." Paisley closed her eyes as though trying to visualize the previous day's events. "I couldn't tell who was accusing whom of what. Something about theft. I assumed money. What else could you steal?"

"And then?"

"Heath tried to strangle Louis. I punched my horn over and over. Employees came running out of the brewery to break up the fight." Paisley shuddered. She tugged her cardigan from her chair to wrap around herself. "Constable Stone arrived a few minutes after it was all over."

"Had Louis lent money to Heath recently or vice versa? Or had he mentioned losing cash?" Motts couldn't think of any other reason for accusations to be thrown around.

"Louis wouldn't have lent anything to Heath, not even a fiver," Paisley insisted. "I can't imagine him borrowing from Heath either."

"What about from the brewery?"

"The brewery?" Paisley paused for several

seconds, staring blankly at Motts before her eyes lit up. "We have to visit Mum's office."

"What?" Motts had barely touched her scone or finished her tea. She wasn't anxious to head to the brewery. "What's in her office?"

"Once a year, Mum did an audit of the brewery's accounts. She picked through it before anything went to an outside accountant for taxes." Paisley began to gather up her belongings, chugging down the last sip of her tea. "What if she found something? Maybe it's the reason she was murdered."

"I'm sure the police checked her computer. Embezzlement is certainly a motive for murder, particularly if your mum intended to turn the facts over to the police or the Banks family." Motts wondered if Paisley realised this meant either Heath or Louis might've killed her mother. "Who had access to the accounts?"

"Mum, Heath, the Banks family." Paisley clutched her purse to her chest. "I didn't. We found a USB drive the day Louis sacked me. I was so distraught I forgot to tell the police. It was hidden in Mum's belongings."

"At her cottage?"

"Yes, but we took it to the office. Neither of us saw the contents, though. Louis sacked me and sent me packing before I could check it on the computer." Paisley got to her feet. "We should go. What if he threw it away?"

Motts ignored the little voice in her head arguing for caution. "Why don't we check the brewery? It may still be there."

CHAPTER TWENTY-TWO

The drive to the brewery went by quickly. Motts texted Dempsey to give him an update. He'd planned to meet her at the cottage later.

When they arrived, the employee car park was empty. Paisley pulled in close to the door. Motts rolled her shoulders, trying to get rid of the uncomfortable sensation running up her spine. She hoped this visit didn't involve running from a tidal wave of beer again.

"Louis shouldn't be in today. His parents told everyone to take a few days off while they sort out who's actually going to run the brewery." Paisley unlocked the door for them. "Fingers crossed he didn't take the memory stick with him."

Making their way through the quiet and dark

building, Motts tried to ignore the fluttery sensation in her chest. Everything would be fine. She had to stop panicking over the littlest things.

She wondered if the cumulative trauma from the past year had left her with an easily triggered anxiety reaction. "Where did you leave it?"

"Here." Paisley rushed over to the desk and shifted around several papers. She picked up the pale pink USB drive. "Oh, thank god, it's still here. What should we do?"

"No harm in checking out what's on it, is there?" Motts stepped around the desk, watching Paisley twist the USB drive around a few times before eventually slotting it into the computer. "We wouldn't want to waste police time if there's nothing relevant to the case."

"Fair point."

They both held their breaths while Paisley opened the folder. It was full of spreadsheets and word documents. One caught Motts's complete attention.

"Financial discrepancies?" Motts pointed a finger at the screen. "She practically put an X on the map for you."

"Should we?"

"Why—" Motts broke off when the door opened and Louis strode into the room.

"Oh. I'm sorry." He came up short after spotting them by the desk. His gaze strayed over to Paisley for several seconds; Motts thought he seemed sad and surprised by their presence. He hesitated for almost a full minute. "Why... actually, never mind, I'll come by later."

Exchanging nervous glances, they returned to the computer. Paisley clicked on the file. Motts didn't immediately understand what they were staring it.

What are all these numbers, and how are they related?

"What are we even looking at?" Motts leaned against the desk while Paisley sat in the chair. "I'm not completely pants at math. Business accounting is a whole other matter. I've got someone who handles mine."

"Mum had her own method for bookwork." Paisley clicked between the various tabs on the spreadsheet. "She obviously discovered missing stock."

"How do you know?"

"There's a notation on this tab about invoices

being received and paid yet no inventory or supplies coming into the brewery." Paisley continued switching tabs, showing the various notes her mum had made. "Someone's been embezzling from the business."

"I don't see any names."

"Maybe Mum wanted to speak with them first? She might've wanted to give them a chance to explain." Paisley closed the spreadsheet. "Or what if it's one of these other files? She put them all on this drive for a reason."

After checking every file on the drive, they didn't have a name. They had two. Louis and Heath both had access to the fraud, since all of the potentially phoney invoices involved came directly from their joint absinthe endeavour.

"Do you smell that?" Motts spun around, sniffing several times. "Is someone having a barbeque? Smoke. There's smoke."

"Oh dear god." Paisley stood by the window looking out into the warehouse.

"Alcohol's an accelerant." Motts had seen a documentary on YouTube about arsonists a while ago. "All the old timber. This place is going to go up like a rocket."

"Beer isn't flammable." Paisley's eyes had gone

wide. She had a hand firmly planted on the wall. "Absinthe definitely is."

Absinthe is alcohol, which is definitely highly flammable.

Motts immediately went over to the door. They needed to get out of the warehouse before the fire got out of control. The handle didn't budge. "Paisley? It's locked. Where's the key?"

"Key?" Paisley stayed frozen by the window. "Mine are only for the main doors. I don't have any of the interior ones."

Brilliant.

Just brilliant.

I'm not flambéing my way to an early grave.

"Paisley." Motts had to practically shout to get her to turn away from the window. "The door is locked. Locked. Unable to be opened. Locked locking locked."

"What do we do?" Paisley rushed over to her. She seemed to finally grasp the severity of their situation.

"We don't panic. You should call the police." Motts didn't think her momentary calm would stretch to speaking on the phone. "And we get out of this naffing room."

Glancing around the room, Motts considered all

of their options. If the fire hit the absinthe, it might cause the blaze to intensify. How quickly could the local emergency services respond?

Not enough to save our lives.

We're going to have to save ourselves.

Motts glanced over at Paisley, who'd dialled the wrong number three times before successfully getting through to the emergency services. "Right. I'm going to have to save us."

Okay.

Take a deep breath.

Dempsey says there's always time to breathe deeply and give yourself a second to think clearly.

What are our options?

The door was locked. Motts knew they lacked the strength to batter their way through the sturdy reinforced wood. Windows. They were on the second floor of the building; odds were they'd survive jumping.

They wouldn't survive an alcohol-driven inferno.

What'll happen to Cactus if I don't make it? Who's going to give him treats in the morning? Make sure he has a sweater on?

Everyone made breathing in a panic far easier than it was. Motts forced her legs to move toward the window. The ground seemed farther than it had when she'd first thought about jumping.

I hope Paisley's not afraid of heights.

"Firefighters are on their way." Paisley had her phone clutched to her chest. "We just have to wait. I grabbed the flash drive. Here. Put it in your backpack."

Smoke had begun to sneak in under the door. They had nothing to block off the gap like people always did in movies. Motts didn't think waiting was an option for them.

"We have to get out now." Motts grabbed Paisley by the arm, dragging her to the window. "Help me get this open."

Working together, they managed to shove the window open. Smoke continued to fill the room. The acrid air burned her nose and throat with each breath.

Smoke killed. They had to escape immediately. The fire had no intention of waiting for the emergency services to arrive.

Over the whoosh of the growing flames and the tinkling bell-like sound of breaking bottles, Motts shouted instructions to a hyperventilating Paisley. Time had already run out.

"Hurry." Motts helped Paisley climb up.

"We'll die." Paisley clung to the frame, unintentionally trapping Motts inside the office. "It's too far down."

"We will sodding die if we don't." Motts yanked up her shirt to cover her nose and mouth. Breathing was becoming increasingly difficult. Her eyes burned as well. "If you don't jump, I will shove you out."

Several horrifying seconds went by where Motts thought she might have to follow through with her threat. Paisley muttered several curses, then leapt from the window. She plummeted from view, landing on the grass below with a pained cry.

Fires were loud. Motts hadn't ever been close enough to one to know. The cracking and popping, the whipping whoosh of flames. Sounds she'd never heard before chased her out of the office.

Dragging herself up, Motts perched on the window frame. She tossed her backpack out and tumbled down after it, landing awkwardly on her back. The ground was far harder than she imagined.

Grass provided no cushion at all.

"We made it." Paisley hadn't moved from her spot several metres away.

With the wind knocked out of her, Motts managed to wave at Paisley in response. She caught her breath after several agonising moments of trying not to panic. They had made it.

We're alive.

"Motts?" Dempsey's voice reached her seconds before he came rushing up to her. He knelt beside her. "Are you hurt?"

"No?" Motts hadn't sat up yet. She didn't know if she'd hurt herself. "Not sure. Think I need a minute."

"We don't have it." Dempsey grabbed her backpack from nearby. "Fire's out of control. The building could collapse. Can you move?"

With a pained groan, Motts eased herself into a seated position. Nothing appeared broken. She got to her feet without too much trouble.

Everything hurt.

"Paisley? Are you all right?" Motts ignored the patient Dempsey and went to check on her. "Can you stand?"

"I've rolled my ankle," Paisley admitted through gritted teeth.

Reaching her hand down, Motts helped Paisley to her feet. Dempsey came over to offer his arm. They made their way carefully around the building to the relative safety of the car park.

"My car." Paisley pointed to the vehicle dangerously close to the flickering flames.

"Hand me your keys." Dempsey leapt into action, moving the car out of the way.

The local fire service arrived, quickly moving to attempt to save the building. Paramedics showed up not long after. Motts pointed them to Paisley, who'd actually injured herself.

They insisted on checking Motts for smoke inhalation despite her protests. Her throat did hurt. She wound up sitting in an ambulance with an oxygen mask strapped to her face and Dempsey's coat draped across her like a blanket.

"Fancy seeing you here." Hughie poked his head into the ambulance. He glanced over at the paramedic who'd been making notes. "Is she up for a chat?"

"Go on. Try to take it easy. I imagine you're going to be sore for the next few days." The paramedic eased the mask off Motts. "Maybe avoid burning buildings, yeah?"

"I'll do my best." Motts stepped out of the ambulance, pausing to take in the damaged brewery. "Holy mother of mittens."

The building had collapsed. None of the

brewery warehouse remained. It had quite literally gone up in smoke.

She couldn't help wondering who had started the fire. It had to be intentional. The office door hadn't locked itself.

Hughie led her over to his vehicle, letting her sit in the front seat with the door open. "Can you tell me what happened?"

Motts gave Hughie a brief rundown of the morning leading up to the fire, including where they saw the smoke first and being trapped in the room. "Louis was here briefly. He left when he saw us in the office."

"Did he now?" Hughie stepped away to have a word with Perry Ash, who'd shown up when she'd been in the ambulance. He returned after a few minutes with the detective inspector. "DI Byrne's going to give you a lift home, if that's okay. Paisley's already off to the hospital to make certain she's not more seriously injured. Perry might swing by with more questions later."

"Fine." Motts didn't argue. She'd had enough of the brewery for one day. "We didn't see anyone else here when we arrived."

Hughie held a hand out to help her stand up. "Try not to investigate if you can. Maybe let us wrap the case up ourselves? I'll bring you over to DI Byrne."

"Sure." Motts nodded mechanically.

I'll do just that.

Right after I find out who tried to turn me into a Motts toastie.

"I'm once again hesitant to leave you here to mull over the day on your own." Dempsey had parked in front of her cottage several minutes earlier, but Motts hadn't quite been ready to move. She'd been lost in thought ever since getting into his vehicle. "How's your throat feeling? Smoke inhalation is never a pleasurable experience."

"I imagine I won't be alone for long." Motts had no doubts her family would be over in droves the second they heard about her close encounter of the flaming kind. "I'll be okay."

"Your throat burns, and your eyes are dry and scratchy. I'll wager your body aches from leaping out a second-floor window." Dempsey followed her out of his vehicle and up to her cottage. "And being traumatised by the inferno likely hasn't done much for you either."

"Oddly observant." Motts was too tired to think of another word for her alliteration. She couldn't deny he'd accurately assessed her state of being. "I honestly want a long bath and a bit of quiet."

Dempsey watched her for a few seconds before nodding. "Why don't you head your friends off at the pass? I can pop by the bakery to speak with them. Alleviate some of their worries so you've space to yourself for at least an hour or two."

With a grateful grimace of a smile, Motts made her way into the cottage. Cactus waited for her patiently. She was suddenly taken back to the horrible moment at the brewery.

"Cactus." Motts knelt on the rug by the door, lifting her purring cat up. She pressed her face against his soft sweater. "How about an extra special treat for you?"

Hugging him tightly in her arms, Motts hid her tears in the fabric of his sweater. She'd been so terrified those last moments in the office. Cactus's warmth anchored her in the knowledge she'd survived mostly unscathed.

A bath at noon was almost as strange as her lack of appetite. Motts couldn't bring herself to even think about food. She couldn't seem to settle herself.

Running a hot bath, Motts floated in the warmth. Cactus stayed close to the tub, watching her with kitty concern. She didn't have the energy to do more than soak in the water and allow her thoughts to drift away.

"Mottsy?"

Motts jolted out of her doze in the tub by a knock on the door. "Give me a second?"

From the cold water and the wrinkled state of her fingers, Motts had been in the tub longer than intended. She climbed out, drying off and wrapping an oversized robe around herself. The bath hadn't done much for her aches and pains.

Bruises had already begun to form from hitting the ground. Motts walked stiffly into the bedroom, where a concerned Vina perched on the edge of the bed. Cactus leapt up next to her.

"You're shivering." Vina immediately went over to retrieve Motts's cosiest pyjamas and thickest socks. "Why don't you get dressed? We'll get a fire going. We've brought snacks. I'll make a nice mug of hot tea for you."

Once the door closed on Vina, Motts dropped onto the bed with a tired grunt. She checked her phone and discovered she been in the bath for almost two hours. No wonder they'd come to check on her.

Cactus patted her face gently, obviously wanting his afternoon snack. He poked at her again. Motts made herself get up and change into pyjamas.

"Ready?" Motts led the way downstairs, freezing halfway into the living room.

Her fireplace was usually a source of comfort. Motts stiffened at the sight of the bright, cheery flames in the fireplace. She closed her eyes and counted to ten, breathing in and out slowly.

"Should we douse the fire?" River asked. "Vina said you were cold."

"I am." Motts opened her eyes to find her three best friends watching her with various levels of concern on their faces. "Leave it. I can't avoid my fireplace forever."

"You sit," Vina ordered before returning to the kitchen. "Tea's almost ready."

Over several cups of tea, Motts recapped her morning. She ignored the tray of treats from the café. Her stomach wasn't ready; her nerves hadn't settled.

"The brewery burnt down. You shoved Paisley out of a window and jumped yourself," River reiterated. "Are you okay? Should you be at the hospital?"

"I'm fine."

Fine might be a stretch.

CHAPTER TWENTY-THREE

"Jump. Jump. Jump, you naffing berk." Motts bolted up in bed, sinking down on her pillow when reality struck her. Her dream had seemed so real; she'd heard the crackling and whooshing of flames. The heat had pricked at her skin. "Right. New worst way to die. Burned alive while someone blocks my way out of the building."

Sitting up slowly after several minutes of trying to fall asleep, Motts gave up on the endeavour. She trudged downstairs. A mug of hot chocolate might help.

It did.

A little.

Five in the morning was far too early to message

any of her friends. She knew they might not mind. They'd also overreact to her fear-driven nightmare.

Grabbing her phone, Motts scrolled through her contacts. Name after name. She saw one who definitely got up early. They definitely wouldn't be annoyed by her text; even so, she hesitated for almost ten minutes before messaging them.

Motts: Are you awake?

Teo: On my second mug of coffee. Hughie mentioned you'd had a rough day yesterday. Guessing your night wasn't much better.

Motts: Fiery nightmare.

Teo: Remember, you're safe now. You escaped, saving yourself and someone else.

Motts: Yeah.

Teo: And you're not alone.

They talked for several minutes until the awkward text silence grew too much. Motts decided to wrap up the conversation. Teo likely had to work, and she wanted to wallow in misery for a few more minutes on her own.

She managed to indulge herself for a good five minutes before her phone buzzed again. This time from Dempsey, who wanted to know if she'd had breakfast. Who had their morning meal at five?

Putting him off, Motts offered to meet him at Talland Bay Beach for an early lunch. She wanted the drive out to Looe to clear her mind. And maybe pop by to see her grandparents for breakfast; her gran and granddad always knew how to make her feel better.

Maybe I should get a car instead of the Vespa; then I could safely bring Cactus with me no matter what the weather is doing.

From the way Cactus followed her around the cottage, he didn't want her to leave. Motts dug around in the cupboard under the stairs to find her cat backpack. Her grandparents would love seeing him.

Dithering around for another twenty minutes, the silence in her cottage finally got to Motts. She got Cactus safely situated in his carrier. She'd ride slower than normal to make sure he enjoyed the trip.

Her granddad was waiting for her by the door after she parked and got off her Vespa. "Hello, poppet. Trouble sleeping?"

Motts shrugged.

"Let's get you inside. I've made tea and toast for your gran. Why don't you and I have some in the garden while your Cactus frolics in the dew?" He waved her inside. "I imagine we'll have more visitors once your uncle sees your Vespa."

He wasn't wrong. The up and downside of living in Cornwall was that family tended to be quite literally just around the corner. Motts didn't mind most of the time.

"Why don't you release your prisoner?" Her granddad came around behind her, poking at Cactus through the mesh on the backpack. "Poor little lad. Has she driven you over every bump between here and Polperro? Let's get you out of here. I've got a little flaky tuna with your name on it."

"His actual name?"

"No." Her granddad chuckled. He carefully eased Cactus out of the backpack, motioning for Motts to set the bag by the door. "Here. Why don't I surprise my Martha with your lad? She'll be thrilled to see him—and you. Pop some bread in the toaster for us. I can hear your tummy rumbling."

The kitchen hadn't changed at all over the years. Motts found herself taken back to childhood whenever she visited her grandparents' cottage. She dropped bread in the toaster, sitting down on a chair in the corner.

"Lemon curd." Her granddad returned to the

kitchen several minutes later, setting a jar on the counter next to the toaster. "Your gran's not quite ready to be awake this morning."

"Makes two of us." Motts got up to retrieve the toast when it popped. They put together breakfast quickly.

"Let's head out into the garden."

Taking their plates and mugs outside, Motts sank down onto one of the comfortable chairs sitting around a stone table. She watched Cactus lazily explore the garden. Her granddad sat next to her, tapping her plate and encouraging her to have a bite of toast.

"How's your throat?"

Motts cupped her hands around the mug, ignoring the toast for a moment. "A little scratchy."

"And your spirit?"

"A little singed." Motts shared a smile with him. He always appreciated her offbeat sense of humour. "I'll be fine."

"Have you had enough time alone to recover?"

"Not quite."

"Just like my Martha. Two solitary peas in a pod." He nudged her plate a second time. "Toast won't eat itself."

"It might if I leave it long enough." Motts

wondered if mould counted as toast eating itself. She took a bite, enjoying her gran's lemon curd, which always tasted better than store-bought. "Did you see the brewery?"

"Burnt to a crisp. The old refurbished barn didn't stand a chance." Her granddad reached down to pet Cactus as he meandered by. "I had a chat with Henry down the street. His daughter does something fancy at the police lab in Plymouth."

"Something fancy at the police lab?"

Her granddad waved off her laughter. "They haven't determined who or how the fire started. They're fairly certain someone used the absinthe as an accelerant."

"I could've told them that." Motts had seen where the smoke first began. "There were loads of papers and wood in the brewery. Any of it would've made perfect kindling."

"And how are your inspectors doing? The London bloke's stuck around for a while, hasn't he?"

"They're not my inspectors." Motts was the one ignoring laughter this time around. "I don't know why Dempsey's stayed so long. Maybe he likes the beach? He said he's working on Jenny's case."

"I'm not sure the case is what's bringing him to

Cornwall, poppet." He got slowly to his feet. "I'm going to check on my Martha. She usually needs another mug of tea before she's ready to face the day."

With her granddad inside, Motts relaxed into the chair. She set her unfinished toast to one side. Her eyes drifted shut while listening to the birds cheerfully greeting the morning.

Loud twits.

Her garden was all food-focused—vegetables, herbs, and fruits. Or, it had been. She hadn't considered the aesthetics.

Her grandparents, however, had the quintessential magical country garden. Her gran had a string of feeders mingled throughout, each one a unique design made by her granddad. Both of them enjoyed watching the birds.

"Motts?"

She opened her eyes to find her cousin peering over the fence. "Shouldn't you be at work?"

"Late start. Mum and Dad are having breakfast with the Bankses to discuss something about the brewery." River disappeared for a moment before popping up once again. "Want some coffee cake? Mum made her special one."

"The chocolate chip coffee cake with brown

butter streusel?" Her mouth watered at the thought. "I could eat a slice."

"You *could* come over here and join me."

"Or you could come over and join me." Motts wasn't ready to leave the comfort of her grandparents' garden. "Why are you at your parents' anyway? Shouldn't you be with Nish or at work?"

"Again, late start. And also, Mum and Dad wanted an early meeting with me before they met with the Bankses." He disappeared for a second time. "I'll be over in a second."

Several minutes later, they sat in the garden, eating cake and gossiping about their family. Motts picked the streusel off to eat first. She laughed when Cactus raced over, wanting to be saved from a dive-bombing bird.

"Ah yes, our mighty hunter returns." Motts shifted to allow him to curl up comfortably in the chair with her. "Why aren't you at breakfast with your parents?"

"The Bankses have *thoughts* about young people running businesses."

"Yet they gave control of theirs to Louis and Paisley, who are both younger than you?" Motts didn't believe it for a second.

River shrugged indifferently. "Or both sets of

parents want to gossip about their children, and I'd definitely be in the way."

"Hard to talk about you to your face." Motts knew her auntie and uncle loved bragging about River. "Have they heard anything about the fire?"

"Not that I heard. I'm sure Mum will share any news with me later. I'll text you," River promised.

Cake, tea, and toast made the morning go by quickly. River eventually left for work. Motts hung around with her granddad, helping in the garden until it was time to head to the beach and meet Dempsey, letting her grandparents spend a little more time with Cactus.

He'd be spoiled rotten by the time she picked him up.

Arriving twenty minutes early, Motts walked along the empty beach. She picked up a few random shells to add to her collection. By the time Dempsey arrived, she felt a million times better than she had.

Being alone with her thoughts and the sea had cleared some of her funk from the previous day. Motts strolled back to the car park, retrieving the picnic lunch her gran had insisted on sending with her. She'd tried to insist they weren't on a date; her grandparents hadn't been interested in listening.

"Are we having a picnic?" Dempsey followed her

to one of the tables that ran along the edge of the beach.

"My gran made us sandwiches," Motts muttered defensively. "There are crisps and slices of coffee cake as well."

"I won't say no to a free lunch."

Sitting on one of the benches at the table, Motts unpacked their lunch. Her gran had included two bags of sea salt and black pepper crisps, one of her personal favourites. The sandwiches were simple BLTs and cheddar and tomato.

"One of each?" Dempsey suggested after eyeing their options.

They ate in silence for several minutes, enjoying the view and cool sunny day. Motts ate the cheddar first and then enjoyed the tomato sandwich, much to Dempsey's amusement. She had a particular way of eating.

"Languishing lazily lethargic." Motts was surprised they were the only ones at the beach. "It's lovely out here today."

"It is." Dempsey finished up his sandwich. "When is Paisley meeting you? You said in your message she'd asked to have a chat."

"In an hour or so. I wanted time to commune with the ocean and enjoy lunch." Motts always found peace at the beach. "Do you have any news on Jenny's case?"

"I'll be returning to London tomorrow. We've a lead on a potential suspect." Dempsey crumpled up the wrapper from his meal. "Try not to stumble into another life-or-death situation if you can."

"I don't stumble into them—I get shoved whether I like it or not," Motts protested. "Have you heard anything about the fire yesterday?"

"Nothing concrete. It's too early for them to have any real details to share." Dempsey selected another sandwich. "They've brought Louis in for questioning. No idea if he's admitted to setting the fire."

Motts suspected Louis had been the arsonist, but she hadn't seen him do it. "We don't know for certain he's guilty."

"You saw him."

"I saw him at the brewery. He wasn't carrying around a lighter, chuntering on about fire." Motts carefully selected the largest of the coffee cake slices. She needed the fortification. "What if he left when he said he did? Someone else could've been the arsonist. I wonder what was on the CCTV."

"The fire destroyed the cameras and the hard drive where they were stored." Dempsey grabbed the last sandwich from the packet. "Hughie mentioned they had to wait for the security company to see if they had a remote copy."

"Convenient." Motts wondered if the arsonist had been attempting to kill them or destroy evidence, or maybe both. "Drive."

"Pardon?"

Motts wanted to smack herself in the head. She'd completely forgotten the flash drive. "I've got to message Hughie. Oh no. What if they think I was hiding evidence?"

"Please stop panicking and tell me what happened." Dempsey reached out to grab her hand, stopping her from crumbling her crumb cake.

Motts grabbed her backpack and pulled out the memory stick from a pocket. "This is the reason Paisley and I were at the brewery. Her mum had this hidden. It's got evidence about someone embezzling money."

"Right." Dempsey gently plucked the slender drive out of her hand. "I'll pop by to speak with DIs Ash and Yuen while you have your tête-à-tête with Paisley. We'll pretend you fully intended to give this to them, but the trauma of the fire distracted you."

Well, I would've eventually handed it over, so it's not a lie.

CHAPTER TWENTY-FOUR

"Where is she?" Motts had been waiting for Paisley to show up after Dempsey headed out to speak with the local detectives.

Ten minutes past the time they'd set to meet, Paisley messaged her. She wondered if Motts minded coming to her Mum's cottage instead. Motts said a reluctant goodbye to the beach and rode across Looe.

Pausing outside the cottage, Motts sent a text to both River and Dempsey, a paranoid reaction to the nagging sensation in her tummy. *Is it paranoia if they've already tried to turn you into a toastie?*

Probably not.

"Sorry about this." Paisley stepped out of the cottage as Motts came up the walk. "I got stuck into decluttering Mum's clothing. If I quit now, I'm afraid I'll never start again."

"Is there no one else to help you?" Motts couldn't imagine how painful Paisley must find the monumental task of clearing her mother's house out. "What about her boyfriend? Or other family members?"

"Just me."

"Can I help?" Motts regretted the offer immediately. She refused to retract it, though, particularly in the face of Paisley's obvious desolation. "I can fold clothes."

Not as well as I can fold paper.

"Would you?"

"I offered." Motts definitely thought she should've stayed in bed longer. "Where do you want to start?"

For the next few hours, Motts helped Paisley box up an entire life's worth of clothing. It was not how she'd intended to spend an afternoon. She chalked it up to doing a good deed.

Cactus was probably wondering where she'd gone. Motts decided to wrap things up. They'd made significant progress, enough that Paisley would be capable of handling the rest by herself.

Despite spending hours together, Motts hadn't

discovered why Paisley wanted to see her. It seemed rude to bring the subject up after an emotionally taxing day. Paisley had been on the edge of tears throughout the afternoon.

How do I bring up any of this without her completely collapsing emotionally?

"Right. I'm sorry your mum died and everything's gone wrong, but can we talk about the fire?"

Dusting her hands off, Motts placed the last pair of trousers into a container. She wanted to go home. Her grandparents were likely worried at the prolonged absence; she should've thought to send them a message as well.

"I'm sorry to eat up so much of your day on this. I can't bring myself to talk about things yet." Paisley led her through the cottage toward the door. She opened the door, gasping in surprise when Louis stood there with his hand raised, obviously preparing to knock. "Go away."

"Can we talk?" Louis's gaze slid from Paisley to Motts. "Both of you? Please?"

I really should've stayed in bed this morning.

"Tea?" Paisley shouted the word, then fled into the kitchen.

With a sigh, Motts gave in to the inevitable. They were having tea with a potential murderer.

What could Louis possibly have to say to them both?

Sorry for almost burning you alive?

The tense, awkward vibe at the table didn't make for an enjoyable afternoon tea. Motts ignored the stale biscuits and barely touched her tea. She seriously regretted not inviting River to come with her.

"Did you actually want to tell us something?" Motts had gotten tired of the façade of small talk.

"I was worried you might be hurt after the fire." Louis's words sounded off to Motts, but she had no idea why. "If I'd stayed, maybe I could've caught who did it."

"How? By catching yourself in the act?" Motts had definitely been out too long. She'd lost the conversation buffer that usually saved her from blurting out her first thought.

"The police cleared me," Louis snapped.

"Did they?" Paisley shifted forward in her chair.

Motts was far more sceptical. She had no reason to trust Louis. "Who else had access to the brewery? Who knew where to find the absinthe?"

"Any of the brewery employees," Paisley offered.

Why do love and lust make people so impractical and illogical?

"True, but we didn't see anyone else at the brewery. No other cars. You even mentioned no one being at work because of the Banks family." Motts tried to bring Paisley down from cloud Cupid. "Louis was the only one there aside from ourselves."

"Heath might've been there." Louis jumped into the conversation again. "I spotted his car coming up the lane when I left. He went past the entrance, so I assumed he wasn't."

Motts suddenly recalled the path leading to the back of the property. If Louis wasn't lying, Heath easily might've snuck into the brewery and escaped without anyone seeing him. "We only saw the emergency service vehicles."

They fell silent for a few seconds. Motts wanted to believe Louis. He seemed genuinely upset they thought he'd hurt them.

Or, more, he's upset about Paisley.

If so, why'd he sack and dump her?

Motts wondered if there might be more to the story. "Why'd you sack Paisley?"

Louis tapped his fingers against his mug, staring into the tea. "I thought the killer might be after her. I wanted to keep her safe."

His story didn't make sense. Motts thought Paisley might be convinced, but she definitely wasn't.

"I'll go." Louis got to his feet, ignoring Paisley's protests. "I'm meeting Mum and Dad to decide what to do with the brewery."

After a second, Motts and Paisley followed Louis to the door. He paused in the hallway, turning to smile at her. Motts had a feeling her presence held him back from saying whatever was on his mind.

"Thanks for at least hearing me out." Louis opened the door, turned toward Paisley one more time. "Can I call you?"

"I—" Paisley's response was cut off by a sharp bang like a firecracker. She screamed when Louis dropped to the ground, blood beginning to show on his shirt by his shoulder.

Time slowed, then sped into fast forward in almost an instant. Motts watched Louis hit the carpet. She saw a figure in the doorway and knew they had to move.

Motts grabbed her arm, yanking her away from the door. "Get back. Hurry."

"Stop." Heath stepped over Louis, callously ignoring the bleeding man on the floor. "I'd prefer not to shoot you in the back."

"I'd prefer not to be shot, full stop." Motts realised Louis had effectively been crossed off their remaining two suspects.

"You shot Louis." Paisley started toward Heath, glaring at Motts when she caught her by the arm. "He killed Louis."

"First, we don't know if he's dead." Motts saw Louis's chest rise and fall. "He's breathing. Second, Heath has a gun. Bang, bang, bang. Death tube."

"Why? Why would you shoot him?" Paisley barely seemed to register what Motts said. She struggled against the hold on her arm. "Answer me."

"He's a double-crossing little bastard."

Double-crossing?

Silence fell after Heath's exclamation, partially driven by his wildly waving his pistol around. Motts mulled over his words. Had the two men colluded together?

Collusion.

Good word.

A Dempsey word.

I wonder if I can get away with texting Dempsey.

From their snooping into the thumb drive, Motts knew the funds diverted had been connected to the absinthe, a project controlled by Louis and Heath. Had they both been aware of the theft? And if so, were they connected to the murder or arson?

Had Louis double-crossed Heath after the murder of Petunia or before? Was sacking him the betrayal? Had Louis wanted all of the stolen funds for himself?

There were so many questions. Motts didn't think Heath wanted to answer any of them. She had to keep him talking.

Talking and not shooting anyone else.

"Why did you kill her?" Motts knew drawing Heath into the conversation might keep them all alive. *What a shame I'm completely pants at small talk.* "Did she go after Louis?"

Maybe he'll believe we think Louis's fully responsible.

Probably not.

"Petunia never knew when to leave well enough alone." Heath pointed his weapon at her. "A nosy bint like you. I saw you poking around the brewery."

"You watched her," Motts guessed. "The binoculars by the wall belonged to you."

"She paced by the window all the time. It let me know when she was up in the office." Heath held his gun loosely in one hand, leaning casually against a wall. He scowled at Paisley, who continued to hover behind Motts. "Your mother ruined all of my hard work."

Hard work?

Is theft hard work?

Well, pirates certainly did their fair share of labour in their endeavours.

Oh, he's talking again.

"Have you any clue how many years I've spent at Coastal Port?" Heath spat out the question.

Motts shook her head slowly. "A few years at least, I'd assume."

"Thirty years. Thirty. Before his blasted family bought the place." Heath waved his gun toward Louis. "His parents kept me on after buying the brewery. They refused to allow me to take charge. I knew the place and the local market. Yet Petunia had control of the numbers. All I wanted was to move the business forward."

And steal from the company coffers.

"Did she threaten to sack you?" Motts wondered.

"I went up to her office after everyone else had gone. I planned to offer her a cut of the money." Heath once again waved his pistol at the prone figure on the floor. "Stupid, pretty boy made the perfect foil. I could've laid all the blame on his shoulders."

"Mum would never...." Paisley trailed off when Louis uttered a pained grunt. She yanked her arm away from Motts, darting over to kneel beside her ex-boyfriend. "He needs a doctor."

Motts found herself the uneasy recipient of

Heath's sole attention. "Why did you kill her?"

"She planned to call the police." Heath shifted slightly. His attention was now split between Motts and the couple on the floor. "What else could I do? Everything was so sodding perfect. She had to bugger it all up for me."

"How—" Motts didn't get a chance to ask about how he'd committed the crime.

Glass broke to her right. A door slammed open on her left, narrowly missing Louis's legs. A cacophony of shouting followed.

In the blink of an eye, Motts was grabbed and physically carried through the shattered glass door into the garden. Dempsey set her down. He checked her over carefully, stopping when she swatted at him.

"Were you hurt?"

Motts shook her head rapidly. "You interrupted me. I was going to find out how he killed her."

Dempsey blinked at her several times, then snorted with laughter. "My apologies for the inconvenience. The gun being pointed at you was more of a concern."

"Louis might've been involved in the embezzlement." Motts wanted to make sure the police knew what had been said. "Not sure about the murder or the arson."

"Let's get you out of here." Dempsey led her through the cottage, past the police who'd detained Heath already and the paramedics working on Louis. "They know where to find you if they have questions."

Riding her Vespa over to her grandparents with Dempsey following, Motts dreaded their reaction. She'd hoped they hadn't heard anything about her long afternoon, but they had if the tears in her gran's eyes were anything to go by.

"Hello, Cactus." Motts lifted him up when he came racing over the minute she stepped into her grandparents' kitchen. He meowed indignantly at her, patting at her face. "I know, I'm horribly late."

"And who's this young man?" Her gran hugged her tightly before focusing all of her attention on Dempsey. "Is this the Londoner? Oh, he is hand-some, isn't he?"

"Gran." Motts flushed with embarrassment. "Detective Inspector Dempsey Byrne. My gran, Martha, and granddad, Jon. They're pleased to meet you. And I should get Cactus home."

Tuning out the probing questions her grandpar-ents lobbed at Dempsey, Motts greeted Cactus, then gently secured him in his carrier. She hefted him onto her back, more than ready to leave. It had been a long day, her stomach was grumbling, and her cottage called to her.

"You take good care of yourself, poppet." Her granddad kissed her on the top of her head. "We'll come see you tomorrow. We can finalise the plans to sort out your garden."

Dempsey followed her out to where she'd parked her Vespa. "How about I follow you home? Make sure you get there safely."

"I'm fine."

"Shock hits people at weird times." He hesitated for a moment while watching her. "I honestly don't believe you should drive. Why don't you leave your Vespa with your grandparents for a day? I can give you a lift home. I'm sure your cousin would help you retrieve it tomorrow."

"I'm fine," Motts insisted, but she didn't feel entirely confident. "You're right. No point in being foolish with my safety."

Dempsey raised his eyebrows at her. "Now you're worried?"

"I was worried before." Motts didn't think she could've predicted what happened with Louis or Heath. "I sent messages to two people when my plans changed. I did try."

CHAPTER TWENTY-FIVE

IT WAS LATE IN THE EVENING BEFORE SOMEONE finally disturbed her peace. Motts suspected Dempsey had intervened. Either him or her grandparents had stepped in and asked everyone to let her rest.

She ignored the knocking initially. Her chair by the fire was comfortable. Cactus had finally settled beside her.

"We brought croissants, Amma's special curry potato pasties, and gossip," Vina called out while Motts watched them through the security camera on the doorbell. "Nish and his boy toy are here. They brought cinnamon raisin sweet buns from your auntie."

"You had me at croissant." Motts opened the

door, stepping back to let them in. "I'm surprised you waited this long to show up."

"Your gran can be right terrifying when she wants." Nish offered her a massive quilt from under his arm. "Amma's softest one. She insisted. She said, and I quote, 'it's too chilly up on the hill.'"

"A hug without a hug." Motts grabbed the quilt, wrapping the fabric around herself. "Smells lovely."

"Amma's favourite scent." Vina squeezed by her, heading for the kitchen, managing not to drop the multiple containers. "I've a special tea blend Taara brought with her on her last visit."

With food and a mug of tea, Motts sat in her armchair with the quilt floating around her like a heavy cloud. The weight of the fabric released some of her anxiety. Cactus clambered up to make himself comfortable in one of the folds of the blanket.

Halfway through her first dark chocolate raspberry croissant, Motts put her friends out of their misery. She recapped her close encounter of the pistol kind. They'd heard some of the story already from Marnie, who'd probably interrogated her spouse for the details.

"I heard Dempsey leapt to the rescue." River wiggled his eyebrows at her.

Motts decided the best option was to ignore his

teasing, particularly since she didn't quite grasp his point. Wasn't it Dempsey's job to leap to the rescue? "Any other questions?"

"How are you doing?" Nish cut off both his boyfriend and his sister.

"Fine," Motts responded instantly. She hesitated for a second, sipping her tea. "Well, I'm okay. Bit shaky. I never imagined having a murderer and arsonist threaten me with a pistol. Croissants make everything better, though. Flaky fruit-filled fun."

"Congratulations on catching another killer." Vina raised her sweet bun in the air. "That's our Mottsy, making Cornwall safe one murderer at a time."

"Not sure I can take full credit." Motts had honestly believed Louis had a hand in the murder. "Heath revealed himself as the killer, to be fair. The police swung into action. I had very little to do with it."

"Clever and humble; what a woman."

Motts rolled her eyes at Vina. "I've sung for my supper. You can all go away now."

After a little good-natured whinging, her friends headed out. Motts hoarded the leftovers when River tried to make off with the sweet buns. She fully intended to enjoy them in the morning with breakfast.

"Have you settled in for the long haul?" Motts had to dig through the quilt folds to find Cactus. He complained quite vocally at being shifted. "Are we sleeping by the fire? I don't think my back's up to an armchair adventure."

The stairs did seem quite far away. Motts hesitated before dragging herself, the quilt, and Cactus over to the sofa. She stretched out comfortably.

"Is this better?"

Cactus responded by once again disappearing into the abundant fabric of the quilt. Motts didn't think he'd be pleased if she attempted to move him again. She settled in while watching the fire.

What a day.

Despite Heath's admission, Motts still had a few questions. She hoped he made a full confession that answered some of them. Truthfully though, she doubted she'd ever understand why he'd done it.

Greed never made sense to Motts, particularly when it drove someone to commit horrendous crimes.

The following morning, Motts sat in the garden with a few leftover cinnamon raisin buns and a large mug of tea. She hadn't slept well. Whenever her eyes closed, she saw the barrel of a gun.

It wasn't conducive to a brilliant night of sleep. The couch hadn't helped. Cactus had enjoyed a night in the living room more than she had.

"Anyone home?"

"Gate's open." Motts didn't bother getting up. She'd left the gate open for her granddad, who'd promised to come over to help her begin work on fixing the garden. "Shouldn't you be on the road to London already?"

Dempsey crouched down to pick up Cactus, who'd sauntered over to him. "I wanted to check in on you first."

"Still here." Motts held her plate out to him. "Sweet bun?"

"Should I feel honoured you're sacrificing a breakfast pastry to me?" Dempsey selected one and sat beside her. "You'll be pleased to know Heath made a full confession to the detectives last night. Louis survived being shot. He's likely to be arrested for embezzlement, depending on how the investigation unfolds."

"What a legacy for the Coastal Port Brewery." Motts wondered if the Banks family would close the business rather than rebuild, cutting their losses instead of continuing. "Have you learned anything new in Jenny's case?"

"Maybe."

"And?" Motts prompted when he went on eating the bun in silence.

"We're waiting on Australian and New Zealand authorities to locate the last two missing classmates." Dempsey popped the last bite into his mouth. "I'll know more once I'm in London. We can only hope they're found safe and sound. It's unlikely the killer flew around the world."

"Unlikely, but possible."

"I've been a detective inspector long enough to know in the mind of a murderer—anything is possible." He got to his feet, gently setting Cactus into Motts's lap. "I better get on the road. Be careful."

"Have they identified Heath's vehicle?" Motts's question stopped him from moving toward the gate.

"No one involved in Petunia's murder or the embezzling drove a pale blue vehicle," Dempsey confirmed what she'd been afraid of. "Heath also insists he had nothing to do with destroying your garden or messing with your cameras."

"Which means...." Motts didn't have to finish her sentence. She had no doubt Dempsey believed the harassment was likely connected to Jenny's killer. "I haven't seen the car again. Maybe he moved on."

"Maybe."

"But?"

"Be careful. Try not to ramble into remote areas. Find someone to go on walks with you when possible. Keep your phone charged and on you at all times." Dempsey glanced at the new camera fitted on her cottage. "And make sure your security system is armed at all times."

Motts nodded. "Of course."

"I'll keep in touch."

After hesitating for a moment, Dempsey headed out of the garden. Cactus followed him to the gate. Her cat definitely had a thing for detectives.

Meow.

"No, you can't go to London." Motts went over to pick Cactus up. "Time for you to head inside. You'll catch a cold."

Carrying Cactus inside along with her plate and mug, Motts double-checked her security system. She put his breakfast out, then returned to the garden. If nothing else, a little hard work would help with her anxiety.

There's nothing I can do about Jenny's case.

Stressing myself won't help anyone.

"Are you in the garden, poppet? Can you give me a hand with the gate?"

Motts went over to find her granddad struggling with a load of tools and bags. "What in the world?"

"Young Hughie's joining us with a load of recycled lumber. One of the local farms is renovating a barn. There's loads of timber that's perfect for our use." He set everything down by the cottage. "It'll take a month or two to get all of the work done."

"Granddad." Motts hadn't intended to move so quickly on the changes in her garden. "How much are they charging for the lumber?"

"Nothing." Her granddad came over to give her a hug. "How are you doing this morning? Fully recovered?"

"I wasn't hurt."

"Not physically, maybe. Hurt isn't always a tangible thing, poppet." He squeezed her even more tightly. "Now, we've time for tea and biscuits before Hughie arrives."

"What about your diet?"

"A few biscuits never hurt anyone."

"Cactus? Where did I hide my phone?" Motts searched the bedroom, trying to find it. She dropped to the floor and searched under the bed. "There you are."

Cactus sat nearby, casually watching her from his bed. Motts had to laugh. He hadn't lifted a paw to help her.

"Thanks for all the help." Motts pocketed her phone. She returned to clear the mess off her bed. "Vina's going to be here soon."

A month and a half had gone by since Heath Miller had been arrested for murder, embezzlement, arson, and a number of other crimes. Motts hadn't kept up with the case. Her involvement had come to an end with his capture.

Thankfully, since Heath had made a full confession, Motts hadn't been required to be a witness at trial. She had not been looking forward to the stress of going to court.

In the past few weeks, Paisley had moved out of Cornwall. She hadn't left a forwarding address, wanting a completely fresh start. Motts couldn't blame her.

The Coastal Port Brewery had officially closed its doors. The Banks family had decided to cut their losses, particularly with their son admitting to being part of the theft from the business. They'd also moved away from Looe.

After healing from being shot, Louis had faced his own charges. He'd spend less time in prison since he hadn't been involved in the murder. She had a feeling he'd leave Cornwall as well once free.

Meow. Cactus brought her out of her thoughts. Motts had spent the morning packing up the last items for a few weeks away from home. She'd already put all of his things together.

"Yes, we're going up to London today." Motts tried not to sound bitter about the idea. She hadn't planned to spend the last two weeks of December away from her comfortable cottage. "I'm sure you'll have loads of presents from your grandparents. Or your granddad at least. You'll get to see Moss. I'm sure Moss has missed you."

Dempsey had sent her a message ten days ago. They'd been in contact several times since his last visit. He wondered if she'd mind coming up to London for the holidays.

She'd said no. And meant it. Christmas in London wasn't what she'd hoped for this year.

Her first holiday season spent in her own cottage in Polperro. Motts had wanted to create her own traditions. She'd intended to enjoy all the area had to offer.

It would be a magical and stress-free December.

And then Dempsey had explained that the Australian police had found her former classmate dead in her home. There were no suspects. A week later, another in New Zealand had died in a suspicious car accident.

Definitely not a coincidence. The Australian police were keeping an eye on the remaining living classmate in Perth. Dempsey had reached out to American authorities in the hopes of tracking down and warning the two who lived there.

Out of all the girls in her year at primary school,

Motts was one of few survivors. She'd reluctantly agreed to head to London for the last two weeks of December. Her parents were thrilled.

Motts wasn't.

The rest of her extended family intended to come up later, for the week between Christmas and New Year's, so she'd have reinforcements eventually. Vina and Taara were driving her up to London. It was going to be a chaotic road trip with Cactus joining them.

"Maybe I should've taken Teo's offer to give us a lift." Motts had appreciated his gesture, but driving down from up north to Cornwall then back to London made no sense. Cactus climbed into her suitcase, curling up on one of her cardigans. "Are you trying to help?"

He wasn't.

Zipping up her suitcase, Motts carried it down the stairs along with her backpack. Cactus followed close behind. She'd had a devil of a time wrapping up the last of her orders for the shop and getting them in the mail before her trip.

She'd also had to cancel a non-date with Beck. They'd been on several in the past month. She still didn't know how she felt about them.

Brilliant friend, maybe more in the future. What

Motts appreciated most about Beck was they didn't push for anything. They'd been happy to slowly build a friendship with no expectation.

The beep-beep of a car horn told her Vina had arrived. Motts went to open the door, carrying out the suitcase and backpack. She left them on the walk, returning to retrieve the rest of her bags.

One for Cactus, one for snacks, and one for presents.

Snacks were critical for staying with her parents. Her mum had a lot of ideas about healthy diets. Motts refused to go without decent chocolate, biscuits, and crisps, even if her dad was fine with making the sacrifice.

"Ready?" Vina asked. She'd gotten out to help with the bags. "This is all you need for two weeks? Talking about packing light."

"Where's Taara?" Motts peered into the window.

"Taara has a last-minute business meeting, so she's going to catch the train up to London. Just you, me, and the tree." Vina grinned at Motts.

"Cactus is not a tree."

"He's also not a cactus," Vina pointed out. "Let's get all this in the boot."

Motts placed Cactus into the car, getting him

situated in the little cat carrier in the back seat for his safety. "He's going to be annoyed within five minutes."

"He'll escape within five." Vina moved bags around, making room for the last one. "What about that one?"

"Snacks." Motts handed it over. "Don't break my biscuits."

"That's what she said."

"It is what I said," Motts agreed. "Have I missed something? Why are you laughing?"

"Never mind." Vina snickered for several seconds. "I brought coffee in travel mugs for both of us. And Nish, bless him, made us sandwiches and macarons for the trip."

"Which we'll eat within five minutes and stop for food halfway to London." Motts planned to take as long as humanly possible to get to her parents' place. "We can play Hobbits for the day. Stopping in a different place for each meal."

"And never arriving in London?" Vina wrapped an arm around her shoulders. "Don't worry. I'll keep you safe from your mum."

"We could always swing by Brighton for gelato from JoJo's."

"Swing by Brighton? It would add an extra two hours at least to our drive." Motts grinned at her ex-girlfriend. "I like the way you think."

They didn't wind up going to Brighton. By hour three, Cactus had definitely grown tired of his cat carrier prison. Motts wanted to stretch her legs for longer than a few minutes. Vina had definitely run out of patience when they hit traffic several times on the journey.

They hadn't even gotten into London traffic yet.

Traffic delayed them by almost an hour and a half. They pulled in next to her parents' vehicle. Her family's semi-detached home in Dulwich hadn't changed much over the years.

"You're going to have to remind me that this is only for a few weeks." Motts reached over to grab Vina's hand, clutching it. "This feels far too much as though I'm moving home again."

"Mottsy." Vina sighed. She twisted in the seat to face her. "I'm going to be staying for a few days just to make sure you're okay. And if things are too hard with your mum, you let me know. We'll get a hotel room or something. Rent an Airbnb. You're no longer a teenager who is stuck with your parents."

"I know." Motts unbuckled her seat belt. "Let's

get this over with. I'm only making this all worse in my head by stressing. Maybe Mum's changed."

Her mum hadn't changed.

Her bedroom also hadn't changed. At all. Motts had fled to it with Cactus and Vina in tow. They'd brought all her bags as well.

"This is weird, right?" Motts couldn't believe her parents hadn't altered anything in the room.

"We've seen weirder." Vina peered around the room, shaking her head. "Possibly. Your mum definitely has issues with you being in Polperro."

"You think?" Motts went over to pick up a stuffed teddy bear on the bed. "Teddy. I haven't seen him in years."

"You named your teddy bear Teddy?"

"Don't judge me." Motts set him back on the blanket. "Should I be concerned my mum dragged out some of my childhood toys?"

"Fresh flowers?" Vina went over to the desk in the corner, lifting up the small crystal vase with a tiny bouquet. "You're allergic."

"Yes, yes, I am." Motts wasn't surprised at the presence of flowers despite her allergies. "Mum believes no room is complete without a floral presence."

"Merry Christmas, have an allergy attack as a present." Vina went over to the windows, opened one and chucked the flowers out the window. She set the empty vase on the desk. "There. Nature back out where it belongs."

"Vina." Motts choked on a laugh. She repeatedly coughed as her eyes watered. "I can't believe you threw flowers out the window. What if it hit someone?"

They nattered on for several minutes. Motts refused to admit she was hiding. She didn't want to go out to deal with her parents.

The road trip had been nice, if long. The destination wasn't ideal, since London had never been a comfortable place for her. She found it far too loud.

"I've got to head out." Vina came over to give her a hug. She played with a strand of Motts's hair. "I'll only be down the road. If push comes to shove, we'll find a bigger place to rent for the holidays, and you can stay with us."

After Vina left, Motts managed to stay out of her mum's way. Her dad hadn't come home yet from meeting up with several friends. She wanted to hide until he arrived.

Meow.

"Hello, Cactus." Motts smiled when he came strolling into her bedroom. "Did you have a nice chat with Moss?"

Cactus hissed when her mum came into the room. He leapt onto the bed next to Motts, who lifted him into her arms. *Well, here we go. This will be a nightmare.*

"Your mangy beast never warms up to me." Her mum came further into the room. "He used to leave hairballs in my shoes."

"I'm sure he...." Motts didn't know what she wanted to say. "He doesn't have fur—he has peach fuzz. How could he possibly have left hairballs?"

Cactus hissed for a second time.

"He adores your father."

"Cactus adores people who love me." Motts considered her words for a moment. "And tall detective inspectors."

"I love you, darling."

"I know." Motts held Cactus tightly in her arms, keeping her eyes on him instead of her mother. "The trouble is you love a version of me that I can never achieve. It's the image you have of what your perfect daughter should be. And every time you realise I can't meet your expectations, you seem to become increasingly bitter at who I really am."

"Darling—"

"I can't have this conversation right now." Motts fled the room, leaving her mother in stunned silence.

Making her way through her childhood home, Motts went out into the garden. She set Cactus down to explore. Her mood plummeted even further at the idea of spending two whole weeks here.

It's going to be a long December.

Maybe I should've taken my chances in Polperro —with or without the serial killer.

Motts glanced down when Cactus meowed plaintively at her. "Not to worry. We'll have a brilliant rest of December and Christmas despite Mum's best efforts."

Meow.

"It'll be great. We'll have pudding and presents." Motts wandered over to the tree at the end of the garden. She sat on the bench underneath, a favourite of her father's. "Pudding, presents, please."

And hopefully, no more dead bodies.

IF MOTTS OFFERED JUST THE RIGHT LEVEL OF mystery and escapism, be sure to check out more cosies from me. Check out the complete GRASMERE

COTTAGE MYSTERY TRILOGY and my London Podcast Mysteries series, starting with **COSPLAY KILLER**. Perhaps you're looking for another autistic female character to become friends with. If so, check out **THE MISGUIDED CONFESSION**.

ABOUT THE AUTHOR

Thanks for reading Pickled Petunia. I do hope you enjoyed my story. I appreciate your help in spreading the word, including telling a friend. Before you go, it would mean so much to me if you would take a few minutes to write a review and share how you feel about my story so others may find my work. Reviews really do help readers find books. Please leave a review on your favorite book site.

Don't miss out on New Releases, Exclusive Giveaways, and much more!

Join my newsletter:

http://eepurl.com/QonoX

Join my reader group:

www.facebook.com/groups/110875087616 2947

I'd love to hear from you directly, too. Please feel free to email me at dahlia@dahliadonovan.com or check out my website https://dahliadonovan.com/ for updates.

Dahlia Donovan wrote her first romance series after a crazy dream about shifters and damsels in distress. She prefers irreverent humour and unconventional characters. An autistic and occasional hermit, her life wouldn't be complete without her husband and her massive collection of books and video games.

 facebook.com/dahliadonovan

 twitter.com/DahliaDonovan

instagram.com/dahliadonovanauthor

 pinterest.com/dahliadonovan

ACKNOWLEDGMENTS

A massive thank you to my brilliant betas who take my first draft and help me turn it into something legible. To Becky and Olivia, who always have faith in me. To all the fantastic people at Tangled Tree. And also to my beloved hubby, who keeps me from losing my mind while I'm stressing over word counts.

And, lastly, thank you, readers, for following me on my writing journey. I hope you enjoyed *Pickled Petunia*. Motts is a character very close to my heart, and I hope you loved her as much as I do.

ABOUT THE PUBLISHER

As Hot Tree Publishing's first imprint branch, Tangled Tree Publishing aims to bring darker, twisted, more tangled reads to its readers. Established in 2015, they have seen rousing success as a rising publishing house in the industry motivated by their enthusiasm and keen eye for talent. Driving them is their passion for the written word of all genres, but with Tangled Tree Publishing, they're embarking on a whole new adventure with words of mystery, suspense, crime, and thrillers.

Join the growing Hot Tree Group family of authors, promoters, editors, and readers. Become a part of not just a company but an actual family by submitting your manuscript to Tangled Tree Publishing. Know that they will put your interests and book first, and that your voice and brand will always be at the forefront of everything they do.

For more details, head to www.tangledtreepublishing.com.

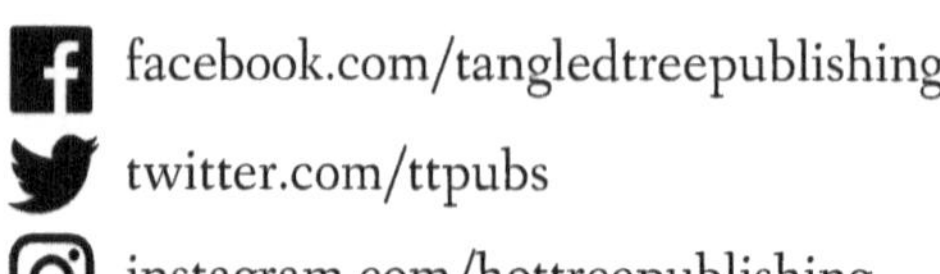

facebook.com/tangledtreepublishing

twitter.com/ttpubs

instagram.com/hottreepublishing